MW00764703

AFTER

E A R T H™

########## KITAI'S JOURNAL

ADAPTED BY CHRISTINE PEYMANI

BASED ON THE SCREENPLAY BY

GARY WHITTA AND M. NIGHT SHYAMALAN

STORY BY WILL SMITH

SKETCHES BY JASON KATZENSTEIN

HARPER

An Imprint of HarperCollinsPublishers

/////////////////////

Library of Congress catalog card number: 2013934065
ISBN 978-0-06-226857-0

13 14 15 16 17   LP/BR   10 9 8 7 6 5 4 3 2 1
❖
First Edition

Today is the biggest day of my life so far: the day I become a Ranger, one of the defenders of our planet, Nova Prime. At least, it better be. Sure, thirteen is young to make Ranger, but I'm not just some kid. I'm Kitai Raige, son of Cypher Raige, Commander General of Nova Prime and the greatest hero our planet has ever known. Seriously—he's the first person to ever single-handedly kill an Ursa, the most perfect hunters of humans ever created. Makes sense, since they were bioengineered specifically to kill us. This alien race, the Skrel, hates us so much that they have been fine-tuning these monsters we call "Ursa" for centuries just to try to wipe us out. No one knows why—we've never gotten any communications from the Skrel, just the arrival of these killer beasts. The crazy thing is, the only way these Ursa can see us is by sensing our fear, since they have no eyes, and since fear is the one trait all humans share. Or, almost all. Not my dad. He literally has no fear. Really. That means he's invisible to the Ursa, which means they can't kill him. What he does, it's called "ghosting," and so far there are only seven people in the world who can do it. They're the best protection our planet has, and my dad is the best of all of them.

It probably sounds awesome, having a dad like mine. Except the thing is, he's not around much, not since I was little anyway. I mean, I get it—he's been Commander General since before I was born, which means he's basically in charge of our entire planet. Technically, we have three branches of government, and the Savant and the Primus help run our colony too. But when we're under constant attack like we have been since the Skrel started sending the Ursa to kill us, the science and religion branches kind of have to take a backseat to the military. My mom is a scientist, so she wouldn't exactly agree with that. But it's the truth.

Today my dad is coming home for the first time in what feels like forever, and I can't wait to tell him that I'm a Ranger, that I'm making progress toward being just like him. It's the only way I can think of to make him proud. Maybe then, he'll finally feel like getting to know me. It's the best chance I have.

Last night, my mom came into my room to talk. Her coat was covered in dust and her hair was wild and windblown. She'd been working up on the ridge all day. She told me there were a lot of orographic uplifts. That's when mountains or other terrain forces air upward. I know things like that because she quizzes me on science stuff all the time. We learn some in school, of course, but she wants me to know more than that.

She hopes someday I'll take over the turbine research division for her. Yeah right.

I get it. She respects what Dad does, but she wants me to be safe, and her work is important too. But I wish she would give it up. Can't she see I was born to be a Ranger? How could the only son of the Original Ghost be anything else? She wants me to believe I have options, but really, I don't. Not while the Skrel are still sending Ursa to kill our people and destroy our colony. Our safety has to come first. That's why the Commander General is the true leader of Nova Prime, not the Primus, who leads our religion, or the Savant, the head scientist. Things like that are fine in peacetime, and I know they help people even now, but they aren't what matters most. I want to—I *have* to—do what we need most. Even if it kills me. Mom knows me better than anyone else, but I don't know if she understands that.

She asked about my Ranger test. I didn't want to talk about it then. Sure I think I passed, but I don't want to assume anything. I told her my plan—to tell the Commander General on Senshi's birthday that I got into the Ranger Program. That's why he's coming home now, so we can all be together on my sister's birthday. I think it would help all of us, if we had something to celebrate on that day again.

Mom reminded me that not everyone makes Ranger on their first try, but that won't be me. I've worked so hard for the chance to make my dad proud. I'm not going to fail now.

I get into my uniform and head over to the Ranger Academy to get my results. On the way there, I pass a statue of my father in the quad, and then images of him carved into the walls of my school. It's weird seeing him everywhere, when I never actually see him in real life.

Not much longer to wait now. My stomach is all twisted up in knots. I shouldn't have any reason to worry.

No reason at all.

want to scream. Commander Velan is the worst Ranger Instructor ever. My scores are better than everyone's, and he *fails* me for it? I can't even believe it. Maybe he's jealous that I'm so good. Maybe he's jealous of all of us Raiges—a lot of people are, actually. Especially the Kincaids, but that's a story for another time. When I'm less angry. Maybe when I tell my dad, he'll see what a dumb decision Velan made, and he'll overrule it. He could, if he wanted to. He's the only one who's *really* in charge.

But no. My dad—correction, the Commander General—would never do that. He trusts his people and he hardly even knows me, so why would he take my word over Velan's? He'll think I'm too young. That I can't handle being a Ranger yet. But I *can*. Maybe if Senshi were here, she could talk to him. . . . But if Senshi were here, everything would be different. Then my dad would still care about me. Maybe he'd even be here sometimes, if not for me, then for her at least. . . .

I'm not gonna cry on this recording. That is not conduct befitting a Ranger—I mean, a *Cadet*. Better try this later.

Okay. Calmer now.

Here's what happened: I went into Commander Velan's office, expecting to be told I'd passed my Ranger test.

He said, "Your test scores are very impressive. In the classroom, you are an outstanding Ranger. But in the field, you collapse."

I couldn't believe what I was hearing.

And then he said the words I dreaded most, "I'm not advancing you."

It felt like a punch to the gut. It took everything I had not to double over, or fall to the floor, or scream in his face. But he kept talking, and I knew I'd better listen. "You are emotionally unpredictable. You have improper threat assessment and you confuse courage with recklessness, which, at the end of the day, is just a far more dangerous way of being scared. You may try again next year. Dismissed."

I was practically hyperventilating. This could *not* be happening. I wouldn't let it. "Sir. Permission to address the Commander, sir," I said, keeping my voice as steady and clear as I could.

"Denied," he said. But when he met my eyes, I thought I saw an invitation there so I rushed forward with my argument anyway. "Sir, I am dedicated, have studied, and consistently displayed conduct becoming of a Ranger. I request that the Commander reconsider his assessment, sir." I stood there, shaking but trying not to let it show as I waited for his answer.

"I understand what it's like to see someone die," he said. "I know what that does to you." I had half-expected a reprimand, half-expected him to change his mind. But I wasn't prepared for empathy.

I felt tears welling up at the kindness in his voice and fought them back. "Sir," I said softly. "My father is returning home tonight. I haven't seen him . . ." I trailed off. I couldn't even remember exactly when I saw him last, but I didn't want to admit that. It was embarrassing to have so little connection to a man who everyone knew. "Today's a special day for our family. And I *have* to be able to tell him that I have advanced to Phase Two. I have to be able to tell him that I am a Ranger, sir." I hated the note of pleading that entered my voice then, but there it was.

He stared at me for a long moment and I allowed myself the slightest hope that I might have gotten through to him. But then he shook his head. "You tell your father that I said 'welcome home.' Dismissed."

He looked down at the next Cadet's file, making it clear that our conversation was over. But I still couldn't make myself leave. After everything I'd done to reach this point, how could it be over, just like that? It couldn't. I wouldn't let it.

Then came the reprimand. "Your lessons in discipline begin right now," he said. "You may leave this room with the dignity and decorum befitting a Cadet."

And so I left. What else could I do?

I knew what he meant, even though I pretended not to. I'm smaller and younger than most of the other Ranger Cadets, so yeah, I've got something to prove. I'm the son of the Commander General, and I don't want anyone to think I got the short end of the genetic stick. But also, I'm good, and I just don't see any point in holding back, not when lives are always on the line. If I'm faster, stronger, better than everyone else, then I'll know that next time I come face-to-face with an Ursa, I can kill it. Before it takes anyone else from me.

I push harder than I have to. To me, that just seems smart. I can see where I may have taken a few risks during the Ranger testing that maybe I didn't have to, a few orders I didn't strictly follow.

Then again, following orders without question can get people killed. If I hadn't obeyed Senshi's order to stay hidden while she fought the Ursa, maybe . . . Maybe

I'll never know, but I do know what didn't work: blind obedience. I refuse to make the same mistake again.

Maybe I do go too far in training sometimes. Maybe. Like, yesterday when we were running, and I raced as fast as I could to make sure I finished first. Bo, the leader of our group of Cadets, told me it wasn't a race, that I shouldn't push so hard. And I didn't listen, because I couldn't. I can't let anyone talk me into doing less than my absolute best, every single time. Good enough isn't good enough, not for me.

It bugs me that Bo got picked as our leader instead of me. Okay, he's three years older, bigger, stronger — but I'm *still* faster and better. He's a good guy, we're friends and all, but I want him to know how good I am too.

When I got paired with him for our rock-climbing exercise, I left my safety harness behind. I climb better without it slowing me down. I ignored Bo's order to put it on and reached the peak without it. At the top, I stood on a fifteen-centimeter ledge with only a sheer ninety-degree slanted rock face above me. I scouted for a handhold and swung out over the canyon sixty-one meters below, using my body's own momentum to swing over and pull myself onto the ridge. Pure exhilaration. Doing it with a harness just can't compare. There I was, literally on top of the world, staring out at the amazing city we have built in perfect harmony with our planet. And all Bo could say was, "That was stupid."

I shrugged, grinning. "They don't give statues for being scared."

Bo just doesn't get it. He doesn't know what it's like to feel your own power that way. And he doesn't understand that I don't take risks for the thrill—I do it because if an Ursa chases me up a cliff, it's not going to wait for me to click into my harness before it comes after me. I have to be able to do it this way, or it's meaningless. But I wouldn't have tried it if I were in any real danger. It *would* be stupid to throw my life away on a training exercise. But just because he can't do what I did, he labels it reckless. And so does Velan.

As we zip-lined back down to the plateau, the view was even more breathtaking. Buildings so at one with nature they literally seem to be an extension of the canyon where they were built. This is our home; this is everything we fight to protect. There's no such thing as going too far when you have so much to lose.

That's why, when we were running an exercise yesterday and I spotted a little flash of something among the rocks, the slightest disturbance in the air, I acted without hesitation. That's all the warning we would get with an Ursa. They're invisible until they choose to reveal their horrifying selves so they can more fully exploit our fear. I broke formation, disobeyed orders. Bo ordered me to fall back, but I didn't listen. If it had been an Ursa, that would've made me a hero. But since it was just training, and I wasn't authorized to attack, it made me a reckless Cadet.

They blocked my vision so the Ranger Instructor could take me out—probably because, even with his cutlass, he couldn't have done it otherwise. I'm not trying to brag, but even with just a training staff, I'm really good. I still fought back, refusing to give in. That's a Ranger to me—someone who never gives up. I know I'm just a Cadet now, but I can't go along with everyone else like some kid playing follow-the-leader. That's not what it takes to defeat an Ursa. It's not what it takes to save lives. And that's what really matters.

I feel bad that my whole team got pulled out of the exercise because of me. I know they were mad. Of course, none of them dared to complain. How could they, when I'm the son of the Commander General? Maybe they talk behind my back, I don't know. Call it recklessness if you want, but it's exactly what's going to save my life someday. Theirs too, I bet. Can't be sorry for that.

I feel like all I've done today is wait. I dressed carefully in my full Ranger Academy formal attire so my dad would be impressed. Mom made his favorite meal and set the table for three. But then we sat silent, staring out at our sparkling view of the city, with a nearby planet and two suns looming in the sky. He wasn't back, and I wondered if something had pulled him away. Mom would never say it, but I thought sometimes he made up reasons to stay away at the last minute, because when the time came, he couldn't actually stand to be here with us. Or *me*. I know he will never forgive me for what happened to Senshi. I can only try to win back his trust. A losing battle, probably.

The wind shifted outside, making the smart fabric sails outside our building billow, and Mom broke our silence to point it out. Of course she would notice it—

wind energy is her field.

Then we heard a sound on the landing outside, and I leapt to attention. It had to be my dad, and I had to make a good first impression. Mom got to her feet too. "How are my lines?" I asked her.

She smiled at me, the way no one but my mom can, and said, "Your lines are perfect." Teasing me, she asked if her lines were okay too.

I shook my head, in no mood for jokes. But she just gave me that smile again before heading to the door.

She opened it to reveal my dad in full dress uniform, kit bag in hand, his dark eyes staring intensely at us. He looked older than the last time I'd seen him, but stronger than ever.

I felt some tension running between my parents at being together again. It can't be easy to be apart for so long. But I was more worried about the moment when the Commander General turned his attention to me. "You've grown," he said. Guess I should be glad he opened with a compliment. But it seemed so generic that it stung.

Standing at attention, I said, "Sir, Cadet Raige reports." He nodded, then walked slowly around me, giving me the full military inspection. I guess I had asked for that.

Stopping in front of me, he said, "Your collar's ragged. You have a crease on your right pant leg, but not your left. Fold crease. Your jacket is improperly fastened. Before you present yourself for inspection, Cadet, square yourself in the mirror. Is that understood?"

"Yes, sir." I couldn't meet his eyes. I committed every word to memory so I wouldn't make the same mistakes again. All I wanted was to impress him, and I had failed.

I caught my mom giving him a look, and he added, "But this isn't an inspection." I thought that might be the cue for a hug, so I moved closer to him. But all I got was an awkward pat on the back.

We sat down to dinner, eating in silence until he

asked about my test. The question I least wanted to answer. I told him I wasn't advanced to Ranger. It was the hardest thing I've ever had to say.

He corrected me immediately. For not making eye contact. For leaving off the "sir" when I replied. I keep forgetting he's much more the Commander General than he is my dad. He wasn't like this with Senshi. I remember how they joked and laughed. He was proud to be her father. That was always clear.

Finally he said, "That's all right. You're young."

Not what I wanted to hear. I'm tired of people acting like my age is a disability. I'm still one of the best Cadets out there. The Rangers need me.

"I ran the canyon eleven seconds faster than you did," I told him. Then I felt silly. Of course that wasn't the sort of thing that really mattered, to him or to Velan.

"Well, if you were ready, Velan would've promoted you. He's a good man. Knows his stuff. You weren't ready." With that, he returned his attention to dinner.

Just like I thought—he would never stick up for me. Didn't care about my side of the story. Thought I deserved what I got.

I stared at my plate, fighting back tears, until I finally managed to choke out, "I'm not hungry. I'm going to my room." I couldn't let the Commander General see me cry.

"Are you asking me or telling me?" he asked in a

voice cold and hard as the canyon's walls.

"May I go to my room, sir?" I asked, biting off the words.

"Denied. Sit down," he replied, and I did.

My mom gave him a look before walking out. It made me feel a little better that she was on my side at least, but with her gone I was stuck there, alone with him. I knew she wouldn't mind if I walked out like she had, but I wasn't going to disobey a direct order from him.

I sat there clenching and unclenching my fists in my lap, wondering when he would let me go. It couldn't have been fun for him sitting there in stony silence, either. Finally, he said I could go. I leapt up from my chair and went to my room. I was so eager for him to come home, and now I couldn't wait to get away from him.

This isn't what I wanted for tonight. Senshi's birthday was hard enough. Shut away in my bedroom, I kept thinking about the last birthday she ever celebrated.

Dad was out with the Rangers, as always, but when she called, he answered. I remember how she and Mom and I sat around the table, with a seat left open for Dad. My sister and my dad talked a little about *Moby Dick*, and then she held up her cake to him, nineteen candles flickering on top. "Dad, you help me."

I grinned, excited for the little trick my sister and I had planned. Dad told her to go ahead and blow out her own candles, but she insisted he help her. Finally, he gave in, leaning forward and blowing—and all the candles went out. I saw the surprise on his face before I leaned into the frame, laughing. I had stood in for him so it would look like he was there with us, blowing out the candles for Senshi. "Happy nineteenth birthday, Senshi," he said. Then we heard an alarm in the background. "I have to go," he'd said.

I know it wasn't easy for him, goofing around with us while he was on duty—but for my sister, he'd do anything. He never would have given in to silliness like that for me. Maybe he didn't want to have those inside jokes with me because it would make it even harder if he lost me too. Maybe he felt guilty that he was gone so much, that his last words to her were "I have to go." Or maybe he just liked her better.

Thinking like that wouldn't do any good. I pulled out Senshi's copy of *Moby Dick*, trying to focus on the words. It's an ancient book from Earth that my father and my sister used to read together. I've wanted to read it forever, but my mom said I had to be old enough. At thirteen, I finally am. I thought, maybe, if I read it too, it might help me find that connection to my father that seemed to come so easily to Senshi. I know it's just a book. But it meant so much to them. It has to mean something to me too. Problem is, it doesn't. Not yet, anyway. The book's so long, and it's weird reading it on paper instead of on my smart fabric screen. But this is the same copy my dad read, the same pages my sister turned. The two of them even made notes in the margins about their favorite parts, and I want to be connected to them any way I can. So I keep reading, even though it's already clear that my dad is not exactly interested in reconnecting with me.

I can't stop thinking of my dad, though. Alone in the guest room in his own house, separated from me by only a wall.

The guest room was never Senshi's room, because she never lived in this apartment. We moved after what happened to Senshi, to a bigger place, on a higher floor, safer and better in every way. But it's the room that would've been hers. We don't talk about it, but I know I'm not the only one who feels it. Especially because it's the room where we keep all her old things. I imagine him surrounded by the pictures of my beautiful sister, and I understand why he doesn't want to be here when she isn't.

I hear sounds from the guest room, and I listen at the wall. I probably shouldn't, but I have no other way to know what's going on. I hear Senshi's name called in an official-sounding voice, cheering in the background. I don't have to hear much more to recognize it as one of her Ranger award ceremonies. I've watched these video feeds so many times that I could probably identify

any of them from a two-second clip played from the next room. I know he is seeing the bounce in her step as she crossed the stage, the light in her eyes as she accepted her award. I know he is looking at her holographic image and feeling how much *less* it is than her actual self. And yet, it's all we have left of her.

Now he bursts out of the guest room, and I hear him walk to my mom's office. I know she's up, working on plans for the wind turbines. Since her office is down the hall, I can't hear what they're saying. Of course I know eavesdropping is wrong. Conduct unbefitting a Ranger, and all that. But then, I'm not a Ranger—not yet.

Their voices are soft and before long, I hear him marching back to the guest room.

I change out of my uniform, leaving it crumpled on my bed. No point in trying to keep it nice since apparently I'm no good at it. I hear footsteps in the hall again, coming this way. Better sign off, maybe pretend to be asleep.

It was my dad. He stood in the doorway, looking strangely uncertain, as though he wasn't sure he should come in. "Pack your bags. You're coming with me to Iphitos tomorrow."

I was sure I must've heard him wrong, but I could see that he meant it. He left just as quickly as he'd appeared and I stared after him, confused but hopeful. Maybe this meant things were finally going to change between us. My mom had probably told him to take me, but I didn't care. At least he had agreed. As I stared out my window at the stars and the nearest planet looming in the sky, I couldn't believe that tomorrow, I'd be flying past them all.

Now I can't sleep, I'm so excited. I've never been into space before. Usually only Rangers travel off planet, and sometimes scientists—but never Cadets. Iphitos is one of our key military bases and research stations, and I'll get to see it in person. If Bo and whoever else got promoted thought they were better than me, this will impress them at least.

I shouldn't have said that. Bo's my friend, and it's not like he has to be. I wouldn't hang out with a ten-year-old, so there's no reason, at sixteen, he should be friends with thirteen-year-old me. But he is. And anyway, what really matters is that this means my dad wants to spend time with me. That's more than I could've hoped for.

I definitely can't sleep now. I guess I'll read *Moby Dick* for a while. It'll give us something to talk about on the ship tomorrow.

//////// ENTRY 4

I couldn't believe the spaceships when I saw them up close for the first time. They were enormous, gleaming in sleek, contoured silver like some kind of sea creature. The hangar they're in is the biggest structure I'd ever been in.

A Ranger who introduced herself as Lieutenant Alvarez told my dad his ship was being repaired, but we could take a Hesper Class-B Ranger and cargo transport right away. The Commander General said we'd go now.

The lieutenant looked starstruck talking to my dad. I know the feeling. She told us, "The boys on board are pretty excited to rub elbows with the OG."

My mom didn't know what that meant, but the lieutenant was happy to explain—"the Original Ghost." That's what the Rangers call my dad.

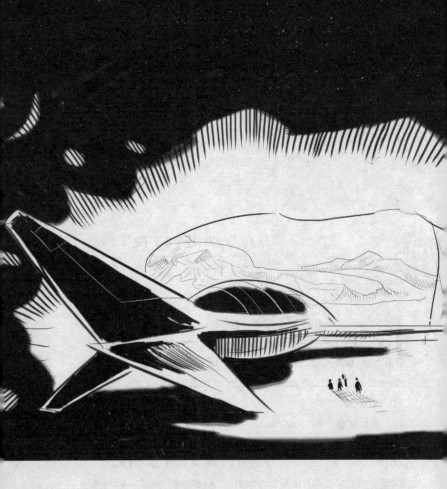

Of course, my dad wasn't fazed by the lieutenant's obvious admiration. You must get used to it, being the Commander General, and the Original Ghost. Turning back to my mom, he explained that he would be supervising some training at the Ranger base on Iphitos. A quick mission, but important for the troops stationed there.

Suddenly, a loud bang rang out, and Dad pushed Mom behind him, shielding her. Turned out, someone had just dropped a tool, but it was nice to see him protecting her. When they hugged, I knew she liked that feeling too.

Seeing them hug for the first time in years reminded me of when I was little and the two of them were so in love, always holding hands and kissing, not caring who saw. I knew it was just a little thing, but it kind of made me feel like we might have a chance at being a real family again. I smiled so big at the sight of them together that my cheeks hurt.

I was watching a giant pod being loaded onto a ship when my friend Rayna strolled over. She's the prettiest Cadet in our class, no question. I can't lie, I maybe have a little crush on her. Even though she's older than me, I think she might like me too. She said she was jealous—not because I got to do Lightstream travel, but because I got to go with my dad. Well, she's right—that is the coolest part, any way you look at it.

My mom headed over to say good-bye, and Rayna said she'd watch our takeoff from the tower. Nice of her to give us some alone time, though I wouldn't have minded talking to her a little longer first.

Mom gave me a long, tight hug. She whispered, "Take it easy on your father. He's a little rusty." I grinned.

That was when a Ranger veteran, being moved to

a medical transport in his wheelchair, shouted, "Stand me up!" He gestured to the two attendants at his side, his magnetic chair hovering just off the ground as he addressed my dad. I'll never forget what he said. "General Raige, I was on the Plateau. You saved me and four others. And I just came from seeing my baby girl's face for the first time." Then he repeated, "Stand me up."

"That's not necessary, Ranger," my dad told him, but the veteran insisted.

The two attendants helped him up, supporting him since he had lost a leg in an Ursa attack. He shook with the strain of staying upright, but still managed a smart salute.

Snapping to attention, my dad saluted back. The respect in his eyes shone so bright—I longed to have him see me that same way. I watched the Ranger's eyes fill with tears. My dad is a hero. Everyone wants his respect. I don't know why these soldiers get it and I don't. I'm his only son, after all. Maybe that's the problem? Luckily, my dad was too busy helping the veteran back into his chair to notice me. I saw him whisper something in the Ranger's ear. I couldn't hear what he said, but I could see that it comforted the man.

This is what the Commander General means to the Rangers. He's a true leader, brave and compassionate, gentle and strong. And this is what he did while he was away from us—saved the lives of his men so that they could return to their families, see their own children's faces. Maybe sometimes he stayed away from us longer than he had to, but then again, maybe he had no choice. He's the best protection our planet has.

He's also the only father I have. Don't I deserve at least as much of his attention as these random soldiers get? But then, I guess that's the problem. All of these men are heroes, and I'm—well, I'm just the kid who let my sister die. So maybe I don't deserve any better than this.

My dad and I followed Alvarez to our ship. The same ship that the giant pod had been loaded into. That was interesting. I wondered what was in there, but there wasn't anyone to ask.

Soon we were flying over the wind turbines and flowing structures of our city, the honeycombed rock faces spotted with smart fabric coverings where our first homes on this planet were built. Before I knew it, we were hurtling through the stars.

I could see my father was scanning a mission dossier, but I couldn't help interrupting him to announce that I was reading *Moby Dick*. I'd been so eager to tell him, but he said Mom had already mentioned it. Then he added, "That's great," like he was trying to care, but didn't really mean it. I guess that's better than not trying at all. I wanted to talk about it with him, like Senshi used to, but I guess this wasn't the time.

I've had so little time with him, I feel like I need to cram everything in at once. I tried to remind myself that we have the whole trip to talk.

The cabin lights dimmed and Dad told me to get some rest. I agreed, but now I can't sleep. This is my first trip into space, and I want to remember every minute. So I'm recording this log instead of sleeping. Disobeying orders again, I guess.

Sometime after everyone else fell asleep, I unbuckled myself and crept past row after row of sleeping soldiers. I only meant to go to the bathroom, but when I realized how close I was to the cargo hold, I had to try to get a look at that pod. I ignored a sign that read *Restricted Area. Do Not Enter. Hazardous Cargo.* I know I shouldn't have, but I couldn't help myself—that sign made me want to keep going even more. I headed down a narrow ramp into the belly of the ship. It was creepy down there, dark and strangely quiet. I slipped past a heavy mesh curtain and into the cavernous cargo hold. I immediately spotted the pod, half-hidden in the shadows. I started toward it, but suddenly a hand clamped around my arm.

"Can you read?" a gruff voice demanded. When I didn't answer, he repeated his question.

Turning, I saw I'd been caught by the ship's Security Chief. Not good. "Yes, sir," I told him.

While he quizzed me about the sign I'd ignored, I peered past him at the giant pod. "What's in there?"

That was when another member of the security detail looked up from a game he was playing with a few of the others. "Might wanna go easy on him, Sarge," he told the chief. "That's the Prime Commander's son right there."

Prime Commander. My dad has so many titles, but that's the most important one. The one over thirty Raiges have held in our history. Prime Commander. The leader of the Rangers. Of this entire planet. I know it's a big deal, but it drives me crazy to have people always acting different around me because of who my father is. But this time, it definitely had its perks. "You're Raige's kid?" the Security Chief asked.

I could see him looking at me in a whole new way, and I puffed up a little with pride. When I asked about the pod again, he offered to show me.

Stepping toward the pod, I paused to guess. "Is it an Ursa?" When he nodded, I asked, "A dead one?" He shook his head, and my eyes widened. Rayna had said something about them catching a live Ursa, but I hadn't really believed her. These monsters were almost impossible to capture alive. But studying the live ones was probably our best shot at figuring out how to finally defeat them.

"This is one of three we caught," the Security Chief

explained. "We keep all three on Iphitos, away from the civilian population. This one we call Viper. She's the biggest and meanest."

Then he issued a challenge, one I couldn't resist. "You want to see if you can ghost?"

I noticed that all of the other Rangers were watching us now. "The pod is biostructural organic armor. She's strapped and suspended in a gel inside there." The chief nodded toward the pod.

Fascination and fear battled inside me as the Security Chief kept talking. He said a lot of stuff, but I'm pretty good at remembering, especially when it's about the Ursa. "All you need to do is step over that red line around the pod. The gel doesn't allow smells at certain distances, but at that distance, it can smell you."

I stared at the red line around the crate, gathering my courage. "You're not scared, are you?" asked the Security Chief. A few of the others snickered, and that was it for me. I couldn't let anyone say they'd seen the Commander General's son chicken out.

"I'm not scared of anything," I announced, keeping my voice strong and steady.

The men shouted, "Uhh rahh!"—the Ranger war cry—in support.

"Don't worry," the chief said, grinning. "Even if she imprints on you, she's locked up tight."

I nodded. No backing down now. But the idea of it

imprinting on me gave me the chills. Once an Ursa imprints on you, it will hunt you down until you're dead—or it is.

"Ladies and gentlemen, the son of the OG is going to try to ghost," the Security Chief called out. "Place your bets."

A few Rangers sitting in the corner actually exchanged money. I wondered which ones had bet on me. Then I wondered if anyone bet on the Ursa.

I stalked around to the rear of the organic pod. Holes in the pod's outer shell revealed the gel inside, but that was all. "I don't see anything," I told them.

"Active camouflage. Photosensitive skin cells change color and texture to match its surroundings," the chief explained. "It only uncamouflages so it can frighten you. So you release more pheromones."

I guess I should've known that from watching it attack Senshi, and from all the studies we've done on Ursa. I knew they could go invisible, but I'd never really thought about why they revealed themselves. Makes sense, though. They need our fear to track us, so the more fear they can cause, the better for them. They really are designed to be the perfect human-killing machines.

As I crept closer, the chief added, "Ghosting is when you don't have a trace of fear in you. Good luck doing that."

"To ghost, you must be so free from fear that you become invisible to the Ursa," the Security Chief continued. "Fear is territorial in your heart. It refuses to share space with any other virtues. You must force fear from your heart and replace it with any other virtue. It could be love or happiness or faith, but the virtue is specific to the individual and comes from the deepest part of that person."

I knew those words well. My dad wrote that, to explain how he ghosts. The Security Chief recited it, but I could've too. I've pored over that manual so many times, trying to learn its secrets—about being a Ranger, sure, but also whatever it might tell me about my dad. But the passage on ghosting doesn't really explain much. You can either ghost or you can't—it's not something you learn. And my dad simply has no fear.

Which meant, neither should I. That was enough to hurtle me over the red line.

"Try to control your breathing," the chief instructed me. "Your blood is filling with adrenaline right now, whether you know it or not. Your heart's beating faster. The pores on your skin are opening up and secreting pheromones into the air, an imperceptible amount seeping into the molecular structure of the gel."

I stood about a meter from the pod, eyes wide, waiting. But there was nothing, and at first, I thought it couldn't sense me. I was just starting to think I had ghosted on my first try when the pod began to shake violently. Through one of the holes, I saw the sickly white skin of the creature as it uncamouflaged. I jumped back as the monster screamed, the same horrible sound I remembered from the day Senshi died.

The Rangers laughed, but their laughter was cut short. Tearing my gaze away from the pod, I saw them all standing at attention, cutlasses at their sides, facing my father. I suddenly couldn't believe I had done something like this and thought he wouldn't catch me.

"Kitai, back in your seat now," he ordered. At first, I thought he had come for me, but then he turned to the security detail. "Rangers, go to Red Con One."

The Security Chief told them to secure all cargo, and they hurried to lock down anything they could. While they worked, my dad led me back to my seat. He didn't seem as furious as I would have expected. I guess he had bigger things to worry about than me right then.

He told me to put on my lifesuit. I struggled to pull on the suit that all Rangers wear—I'd never worn one before, for one thing, and I felt weird getting dressed right in the middle of the ship. I managed to wiggle my way into the slippery material, hoping I hadn't put it on backward or anything. I tried to ask my dad what was happening, but he didn't answer. He just ordered me to get into full harness. While he headed for the cockpit, I sat strapped in my seat with no idea what was happening. I watched Rangers securing the cabin, shouting out things like "Left rear secure!" "Cargo hull check!" and "Right zero locked." I only knew what some of that meant. Peering out the window into the darkness beyond, I tried not to let the fear swallow me.

Or the guilt. I had no idea what was wrong, but could it have something to do with me waking the Ursa? Maybe the ship wasn't made to withstand the kind of violent thrashing that the giant beast had done when it caught my scent? Okay, that didn't make sense, not for a ship made to travel through space, but the timing of all this made me feel like I was being punished somehow, for stepping out of line.

And then I felt the impact. I saw wave after wave of asteroids strike the ship, tossing it around like it was a toy. I grabbed onto my seat as the entire ship shook. Muscles tensed, I braced myself. This was so much bigger than me, so much worse than I had imagined, that the guilt disappeared, replaced by pure survival instinct.

Alarms sounded throughout the ship as bigger and bigger asteroids pounded against the hull. We tipped dangerously from side to side and I gripped my seat even harder, feeling its edges bite into my palms.

"Caution. Critical hull damage," blared the voice of the onboard computer. "Caution. Main power failure."

All I could do was sit there, like my dad told me to, hoping that everything would be okay and trying not to completely freak out.

Something big hit the tail of the ship. Hard. It swung around wildly, knocking the breath out of me. Before I could recover, something bigger hit us even harder, shaking the whole ship again. I was starting to hyperventilate. It took everything I had not to unsnap my harness and run after my father. I wanted to feel like I was doing *something*. I hadn't felt this helpless since that day with Senshi: a little kid hiding while an Ursa tore through our apartment, my sister trying and failing to defeat it. I hunkered down in my seat while the captain tried and failed to keep asteroids from ripping our ship to pieces. Both times, I did nothing—except follow orders.

Another asteroid knocked us sideways, and I heard the screech and tearing of metal. That could only mean something major had broken. I had never been in a ship like this before, but even I knew that meant we were going to crash. No one screamed. Rangers are all trained better than that. But I think we all, in that moment, braced ourselves for the end.

And then a blinding white light flashed outside the windows. We rocketed forward, so fast that I was pinned back against my seat. At first I thought this was what death looked like, but then I remembered our science lesson on space travel. This was what my teacher said a wormhole was like. Someone— the pilot? My dad?—must've decided it was our best chance to reach a place we could land.

Suddenly, we burst into a peaceful stretch of winking stars. Through the window, I saw pieces flying off of our ship. This was not going to end well.

Then the navigator's voice came over the speakers. "Cabin pressure dropping, heavy damage to outer hull. Breach possible in middle cabin." The Rangers sprang into action, doing their best to reinforce the cabin. I wanted to help, but my father—the Commander General—had ordered me to stay put. I didn't want to get in his way.

I gasped for breath, and a Ranger handed me an oxygen mask before exiting to the rear of the cabin. I was shaking with fear. This ship was going down and there was not one thing I could do to stop it, or to make sure I would survive when it did. I hated the thought of dying a Cadet and not a Ranger. I hated the thought of my mother losing another child. But it didn't matter how I felt. There was nothing I could do.

A blue-and-green planet appeared in the distance, and our ship careened toward it. We whooshed past a small space buoy, and its recorded message began playing on a loop: "Warning. This planet has been declared unfit for human habitation. Placed under

Class-One Quarantine by the Interplanetary Authority. Under penalty of law, do not attempt to land. Repeat, do not attempt to land." It played so many times that I had no trouble memorizing every word.

I heard the pilot shouting over the radio. "Mayday, Mayday, this is Hesper-Two-Niner-Niner heavy in distress! We took heavy damage from an asteroid storm and are going down with bingo power! Request immediate rescue, repeat, request immediate rescue!"

The main cabin shuddered so violently I thought it would break apart. I saw my dad steadying himself, his respirator face mask in place, as he made his way from the cockpit back to me. As bad as things were, I still felt relief wash over me. With my dad here, nothing could go wrong. He was Cypher Raige, the Original Ghost, Commander General of Nova Prime.

Despite the ship's shaking, all the Rangers were working to reinforce the bulkhead area as warning lights flashed above them. Their military training was obvious in every precise movement. But I found myself wondering if that would be enough.

I wanted to help, but my dad pressed his hand to my chest, keeping me in place. He helped me fasten my belt and harness, pulling them tight. I locked eyes with him, feeling the calm still radiating from him. I had no idea how he could remain calm. I wondered if this was how you ghosted, if this was the secret. And then my dad was slammed into the corner of the main cabin, and I finally released the scream I'd been holding back as he was tossed around like a rag doll. The squeal of splintering metal ripped through the cabin, and I clapped my hands over my ears to block it out. It didn't help. Our ship was being torn to shreds. Dad was whipped to the front of the ship and out of sight. I shouted for him, but the howling of the wind drowned out my voice.

Our ship broke in two. High-pressure air rushed into the cabin. The two halves of our ship fell away from each other. Twenty Rangers, still struggling to solder the ship back together, spun away with the rear section of the ship. The ship continued to break apart as we fell. I struggled to remain conscious, but the g-force was too much for me. Everything went black.

When I woke up, the world had tilted around me. Cords dangled from the ceiling at random angles. I heard the quiet hum of the ship's computers and, in the distance, a buzz that might have been insects. I tried to sit up but my double harness pulled me back. I fumbled with the buckles, finally managing to release them. Stumbling to my feet, I swayed in the aisle.

Then my training kicked in: assess your condition. I ran through my symptoms: dizzy, groggy, confused. I understood that I was in shock, but I didn't know how to snap myself out of it. I just knew I had to find my dad.

A few shafts of light sliced into the cabin through the passenger windows and the gaping hole where the rest of the ship used to be. Past where the ship now ended, I could see some kind of cavern outside.

My breath fogged my oxygen mask and I pulled it down around my neck, trying to get my bearings. I immediately gasped for air. A digital meter on my mask read *Low Oxygen: 15%. Caution*. I yanked the mask back on and took a deep gulp. Relief. I tightened my mask before heading down the aisle to see what else was left.

I saw a body tangled between the seats, too twisted to be alive. I stared in horror at the Ranger, but despite the tight knot of fear coiling in my stomach, I forced myself to keep going. I couldn't stay here. I had to find my dad.

Debris cluttered the aisle, and I did my best to avoid the sharp metal shards. Suddenly I heard a loud beep, followed by a bang and a buzz. I turned to see what it was as two sets of air lock doors began to close. They banged against a Ranger who lay lifeless between them. I saw that his arm was stuck, but the doors kept pushing against him, beeping and buzzing as they struggled to close. The computer's voice blared: "Remove obstruction. Remove obstruction." I wanted to run, but I wanted the sounds to stop too. And I couldn't let the doors keep crashing into that Ranger. He deserved better. Making my way toward him, I nudged him past the doors with my foot until he was clear. He probably deserved better than that too, but it was the best I could do. I had never touched a dead body before. I couldn't handle anything more than that, not yet.

The doors slammed closed and the alarms stopped blaring. A suction sound followed, and air blew hard through the vents. "Repressurizing complete," the computer announced. Now I could take off my mask.

Peering into an adjacent corridor, I spotted a hand that I immediately recognized as my dad's. I rushed over and pulled a piece of debris off of him. He lay on the ground, his legs pinned beneath a fragment of the ship. I struggled to lift it, but it was too heavy. Looking around for help, I saw a long metal rod that had fallen from the ceiling. Wedging it between the ground and the debris to make a lever, I pushed with all my strength. Finally, the large piece of metal lifted off of his legs. I edged it away until it tipped over away from my father, slamming into the floor so hard that the ship shook again.

As I knelt beside my dad, I was relieved to see his breath fogging his face mask—just a little, but better than nothing. I curled up on the floor beside him, watching for even the slightest movement. Maybe I was still in shock, because I couldn't seem to think of anything else to do. But my dad—my big, powerful, heroic dad—just lay there, motionless. I couldn't help it—I started to cry.

I tried to get control of myself, but I couldn't. Was

I really going to have to watch my father die, just like I did with my sister? I didn't think I could go through that again.

I will never, ever, ever forget that day. I was playing Ranger in my room when the air raid siren ripped through the city. I ran to the window and looked down at the walkway two stories below, trying to see what was happening. My first thought was Ursa, but there had been other emergencies in our colony too. Then I saw Senshi, my sister, running through the crowd of people who were rushing back to their own apartments. I knew she was coming for me.

When she burst into my room, I was struck as always by how strong she looked, dressed in her rust-colored Ranger uniform, her cutlass in her hand. At nineteen, she was so much more grown up than eight-year-old me, but she never treated me like I was a baby. She was my hero, my best friend, the most amazing girl in the world—everything a big sister should be.

She shouted that we had to go. We heard a screech so awful it seemed like even the sound of it would tear me to shreds. I covered my ears, wanting to hide. I knew what that sound was without asking. It was an Ursa, and it was coming for us.

Senshi said the Skrel had surprised us, sending ships to drop those monsters on us again. There was supposed to be an early-warning system in place, but somehow the Skrel had found a way around it. I remember her asking if I was afraid. I tried to tell her I wasn't, but I couldn't fool her. I was terrified.

Another unearthly shriek tore through the air, even closer now. I scrambled beneath the hammock where I had always slept. Scooting into the corner to make room for my sister, I called out to her, thinking we could hide together until reinforcements arrived.

But of course, that was never an option. Not for my sister, not for any Ranger. Rangers are sworn to protect the planet, especially from Ursa. As I watched, Senshi spotted the glass greenhouse where I'd been growing plants beneath my window. She hit a button and the round container slid open. Attaching her cutlass to her back to keep it out of the way, she started yanking my plants out, scattering dirt, leaves, and roots until the box was completely empty. I still didn't understand what she was doing, but if destroying my indoor garden would somehow help us, I wasn't about to complain.

"Climb in here, okay?" she said, sliding the box toward me. As I crawled in, she explained that it would shield my scent from the Ursa. They are drawn to our fear, and I knew I was drenched in mine. I couldn't stop it, couldn't conceal it, couldn't ghost like our dad. I knew it, and so did she.

Once I was inside, she handed me the remote that

controlled the lid. "You use this when I tell you to. Or when another Ranger tells you to. Other than that, don't come out. No matter what." I opened my mouth to protest but she shook her head. "That's an order."

It was a direct order from a Ranger. Everyone on Nova Prime knows you don't disobey those. From inside my glass box, I felt far away from my sister, so powerful with her cutlass strapped to her back, ready for battle. But then she leaned in, cupping my chin in her hand, her enormous brown eyes searching my face. "Did you hear what I said, little brother?"

Of course I did. I will never forget her words. They changed my life forever.

I saw the depth of feeling in her eyes, but her voice was as cool and sharp as her cutlass's blades, leaving no room for argument. Her eyes were my sister's, but her voice was a Ranger's. Another screech sliced through the room, so much closer this time, and she quickly sealed me in the case.

I watched as she stood and pulled the cutlass from her back. She tapped out a pattern on her weapon, the C-30 cutlass, and it morphed into a two-meter-long, double-ended, razor-sharp sword. Then I saw a hulking shadow pass across the wall to the next room. Senshi saw it too.

Spinning her cutlass in her hand, she crept into the other room. And there was the Ursa, directly in front of her. All I could see was the bottom of its muscular six-legged body as my sister advanced on it. I heard furniture crashing aside as the Ursa dodged her cutlass. She wielded her weapon like the natural fighter she was, but I never saw her connect. Then one of the beast's massive arms lashed out at her. She leapt into the air, pushing off the wall to escape, but the monster's next blow connected, throwing her across the room.

I clapped my hands over my mouth to keep from screaming.

That thing was hurting my sister, and I wanted to stop it, *needed* to stop it. But as I tried to think of some way to help, fear held me frozen in place. Fear—and the thought of how angry Senshi would be if I disobeyed her orders, even if it was to try to save her. So I stayed hidden. Just a frightened little kid.

The creature pounced on her again, and I heard her cry out, "Dad," in a voice so full of pain that it broke my heart. And that's when the anger began to well up in me too, because I couldn't save her but *he* could have. And where was he when we needed him most? Far away, saving other people I'm sure, but leaving his own children unprotected and alone.

I couldn't see her past the Ursa's massive body, but I heard its claws and teeth slashing and ripping. Finally the monster backed away, and I caught a glimpse of her lying still in the corner of the room. Shaking and sobbing, I fought to stay silent until the creature was gone.

My sister was dead, and I felt like I was dying too. Maybe I should have leapt to her defense, just to spare myself from living with the unbearable pain of watching her die. But I couldn't have done that to her. If there were one thing my sister would've wanted, however and whenever she died, it would be to know that her baby brother was safe. I know that for sure, because I knew her. I loved her more than anything—but she loved me even more. That was why she came here as soon as the Ursa landed, because if she could save one person in the world, it was me.

Senshi used to tuck me in at night, when Dad was away and Mom was working late. And when I couldn't sleep because I was afraid of monsters, she would say, "If an Ursa gets in here, it'll never have a chance to get you. I'll just walk right up to it and cut it down." At least she had been right about the first half of that vow. She always promised to protect me, no matter what, and she had kept her promise—and I had let her.

I wish I had been older and stronger that day so I could have saved her. I replay the scene in my head at least once a day, trying to imagine how it could have gone differently. Maybe if I had snuck up on the beast, I could have killed it while it was trying to kill her. Sometimes that seems possible, and other times, I can see the monster whirling to kill me while my sister lay dying and can see the devastation that would've been in her eyes, knowing that she died for nothing because the Ursa got me too.

We would've made an unbelievable team some-day—the two children of Cypher Raige, fighting Ursa side by side. I can see it so clearly even though we never got the chance. I miss her so, so much. And I know if anyone misses her as much as I do, it's my dad. But the thing that should have brought us even closer together drove us apart. She was his favorite, and I was just the one who let her die.

'm back now. I needed a break after that last recording. Reliving that day always destroys me. I probably shouldn't have even gotten into all that, not when there's so much else going on. But that's what's pretty much always on my mind.

Anyway. Night had fallen while I was lost in my memories, and still my dad didn't move. I was trying to decide what to do next when his eyes finally opened.

My dad calmly surveyed his surroundings. Seeing me breathing without my mask, he removed his own.

He told me to stand up and evaluate my condition. I rolled my wrists, flexed my elbows, rotated my shoulders and neck. I leaned side to side, front to back, squatted up and down, testing my knees and legs. Even though it didn't seem like the most urgent thing to deal with right now, knowing that I was good to go made me feel better.

My dad gave me a once-over to confirm that I was okay. With that done, he told me to make sure the Ursa was contained.

That's when I realized he hadn't seen the rear of the ship rip off. Voice shaking, I told him the news. "It's gone. The whole back of the ship is gone."

"Rangers! Count off!" my dad shouted, his voice booming through the main cabin. But its echoes were met with total silence. A coughing fit overtook him, but when he recovered, he repeated his order.

"Most of them were in the back when the tail broke off," I told him. It felt strange, knowing more about what had happened than my dad did, even for a minute.

Dad tried to pull himself to his feet, but I could see right away that his legs couldn't hold him up. He cried out, collapsing back to the floor. I saw him struggling to stay focused despite the pain. It only took a moment before he was back in control. "The cockpit is directly above us. Go. Now."

I didn't want to leave him. Not when he was so badly hurt, not when he had only just come back to me. I slowly got to my feet, but then I stood there just staring at him.

"Go, Kitai," he insisted, and I nodded. I headed up toward the cockpit. With each step, I felt more and more certain that my dad would save us. He was, after all, the greatest hero Nova Prime had ever known. Maybe that sounds like bragging. But I always thought, it's not bragging if it's true. It would take more than a spaceship crash to take him out.

I drew in a sharp breath when I entered the cockpit. Both the pilot and the navigator were still in their chairs, but they'd been crushed beneath a structural beam. I had to lean over them to see the control board. Emergency lights flashed everywhere. I glanced into the open avionics system just off the cockpit and saw that most of the equipment there was still lit up. At least not everything was destroyed.

"Go to the control board." My dad's voice came from the bottom of the stairwell. "In front of the left seat. Top row, fourth from the right. Activate Exterior Motion Sensors."

I reached for the panel, but my hands were shaking too hard to activate the screen. I clamped them together to stop them, drawing in deep breaths. Trying again, I found the screen for the exterior motion sensors. I hit a button and *Motion Sensors Activated* appeared on the screen.

"Check," I called down to my dad.

Next he told me where to find the emergency beacon and what it would look like. "We need it to send a distress signal," he explained. "Bring it to me."

The thought of activating a beacon and having the

Rangers come save us, wherever we might have landed, made me feel instantly lighter. We weren't trapped here. I would find the signal, press a button, and just wait for our rescuers. Then we'd go home.

But when I got to the communication rack, I saw the damage. I found the emergency beacon, but the bottom of it was crushed. I carried it back down the ladder to show it to my dad, hoping that the part that was broken wasn't the part that mattered.

My dad inspected the damage, then switched the beacon on. Its activity light stayed off. He detached its mangled lower section, and I thought he might be able to fix it. But after a few minutes, he shook his head. The beacon was useless.

I knew it would still be okay, though—he was the Commander General, and he would come up with a solution. I could actually see him thinking, rapidly concocting and rejecting ideas until he reached a decision.

"We need to get me into the cockpit," he announced. "There's a cargo loader at the rear."

I spotted the flat hydraulic machine on a cargo elevator by the ship's front bow. A small ramp ran from the loader to the floor. When I hit a button, the ramp started moving like a conveyor belt. My dad braced his arms at his sides, and I lifted his leg onto the belt. When he winced, I paused, realizing he was in more pain than he was letting on but of course he wouldn't tell me how bad it was. The loader started dragging him up, and I hurried to lift his other leg onto it. With some maneuvering, he was able to get his upper body onto the conveyor belt himself.

When he reached the top of the loader, I saw that blood from his legs streaked the ramp. His blood was on my hands too, from where I had grasped his legs to move them. I could see that he was injured, of course, but those bright red streaks really brought it home. Cypher Raige was not invincible. He was a man like any other. And that meant he could be broken.

But that didn't mean he would stop. I pressed a button and the cargo elevator began to rise. I craned my head back so I could keep my eyes on him.

"Inventory up. Full assets. Now," Dad called down. I paused, noticing that the windows outside were crusted with ice. I didn't find that encouraging. But I couldn't keep my dad waiting while I worried about the weather, so I climbed up after him.

It only took me a second to realize that I was going to have to move the pilot and the navigator so my dad could get to the controls. Bracing myself, I dragged the navigator out of his seat and over to a hatch in the floor labeled *Nitro Storage Container*. It was awful, clutching his cold arm, hefting his dead weight, but I couldn't let myself stop. I hadn't known this man, but I felt grief wash over me at the thought that he would never again fly, or smile, or see his family. But my responsibility now was to the two of us who had survived. I needed to get the bodies into the nitro container to avoid attracting whatever predators were on this planet. I popped open the hatch and pushed the navigator into the container, quickly closing it behind him. I wanted to break down right then, but there was no time. I had to move the pilot too.

Shaking, I turned to see my dad sitting in the navigator's seat. He had transferred himself from the loader to the chair and now sat upright with his left leg propped on the console beside him. Since he was settled in at the control center, I took a minute to get ahold of myself. Sinking to the floor, I tried not to remember the heft of those bodies, tried not to think about who they had been, and who they had left behind. I rocked slowly back and forth, trying to calm my mind. And there in front of me was my dad, bleeding but completely in control. Maybe I really wasn't like him at all.

Dad placed his palm on a terminal to activate the cockpit computers. They burst to life, and I felt a flicker of hope. A hologram flashed the words *Identity Verified: General Cypher Raige*, and the computers booted up. Although the console in front of the pilot's seat was completely destroyed, the holographic display in front of my dad spit out initial readings, apparently fully functional.

He ran through the various systems, and the computer announced, *Main cabin breach. Self-sealing in progress*, and, *Transport ship: condition critical*.

"General Cypher Raige," he said, glancing at the cockpit recorder to confirm that it was capturing his words. "Crash-landed."

Even though the reports were all bad, watching him go through the standard checks helped me calm down. If he could keep doing his job, I figured I could too. So I got to my feet and went looking for whatever supplies I could find. We would need them.

I managed to accumulate a decent pile. A med kit and my dad's kit bag were the best finds. But now the scavenging was done, and I was at a loss again.

"I need you to focus right now," my dad told me. "Assets?"

"Four bodies. I put them in the nitro compartment." Not exactly an asset, but it seemed like an important part of my report. "Radio nonoperational. Four Ranger packs. Cabin pressure stable. One emergency med kit. And I got your bag from the troop bay." I could feel him watching me, assessing my every word and movement. I wasn't sure what he was looking for, exactly, but it seemed safe to assume I wouldn't measure up.

But he just flipped through a few screens until a holographic image of a landscape appeared over the control console. Tons of wavy lines showed the contour of the land, with a blinking light in the midst of it.

As Dad stared at the image, I saw his mouth tighten, uncertainty flashing for the first time in his eyes. Then he drew in a deep breath, and he was the Commander General once more. Whatever he had decided, I knew I would have to obey. "Hand me the med kit and Ranger pack," he ordered.

I retrieved both and handed them to him. He grabbed my wrist and activated the naviband on my lifesuit. Data from the band appeared in layers around my wrist, like a holographic bracelet. I stared at it, amazed. I had always known I would get a naviband when I made Ranger, but I'd never seen one close up. It was even cooler than I could've imagined.

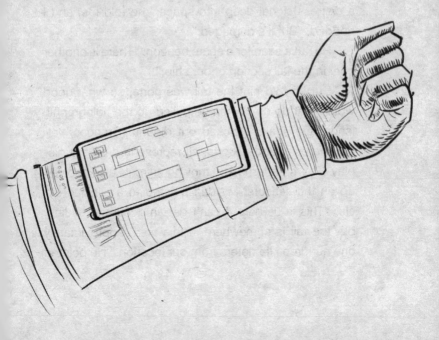

The monitor beside my dad filled with numbers and graphs that matched the ones surrounding my wrist. I realized that he was syncing me with the cockpit computers, but I still didn't know why.

"Cadet. Center yourself," he said, and I used the breathing techniques and mental exercises we had learned at the academy to calm myself as much as I could. I knew he was checking my heart rate to monitor my anxiety level.

My dad sat back and stared at me intently. We both knew how much trouble we were in. We both knew only he could hope to get us out of it. And we both knew he wasn't going anywhere without medical attention.

"The emergency beacon you brought me will fire a distress signal deep into space," he told me, and I nodded. "But it's damaged."

He ran a scan for a spare beacon. "There is another one, in the tail section of our ship."

But I'd told him the tail was gone, so what good would that do us? When he pulled up the holographic landscape again, I picked out mountain ranges, valleys, forests, and deserts, all represented on the display. Storm patterns and moving animals also showed up on the sensors. My dad pointed to a blinking circle. "This is us here. I can't get an accurate reading, but the tail is somewhere in this area, approximately one hundred kilometers from our location." He pointed to a dark section of the landscape where the sensors weren't picking up much. Another blinking dot marked the tail there, but without the details around it, it wasn't much help.

"We need that beacon," he said, and that was when I finally understood. Tears sprang to my eyes, and I tried to swipe them away—too late. I saw that he had seen. But he spoke with kindness, like the father I longed for, not the Commander General I had come to expect. "Kitai, both my legs are broken. One very badly. You are going to retrieve that beacon or we are going to die. Do you understand?"

I could only nod. If that was what I had to do, I would try my best. But for the first time since I became a Cadet, I doubted my abilities. I saw tears welling in his eyes too, and hid my shock. I simply wiped my eyes and awaited my orders.

Dad opened a small black case from the med kit marked *Universal Air Filtration Gel—Emergency Use Only*. Six vials were lined up inside.

"You have air filtration inhalers," he explained, holding up a vial. "You need to take one now. The fluid will coat your lungs, increase your oxygen extraction, and allow you to breathe comfortably in the atmosphere." He showed me how to use the inhaler, and I repeated his movements, bringing the vial to my lips, pressing the release, and drawing in a deep breath.

"You have six vials. At your weight, that should be twenty to twenty-four hours each. That's more than enough." He pressed a button on my naviband, and a holographic map appeared again. "Your lifesuit and backpack are equipped with digital and virtual imaging," he explained. "So I will be able to see everything you see, and what you don't see." After helping me into the Ranger backpack, he activated my rear-facing backpack camera, then tapped a control on the console so the feed appeared on the monitor in front of me. The monitor showed his face as he promised, "I will guide you."

Then he shut the monitor down, and I turned to face him. "It will be like I'm right there with you," he said. I nodded, but I'm sure I looked unconvinced. Having my dad watch my back would be great, but he wouldn't be able to help me fight off anything that might be out there, and I wasn't used to fighting alone. Then he offered me the best tool he had. "Take my cutlass."

He held it out, but I just stared at it in awe. General Cypher Raige's cutlass, the most advanced one ever made. "Go on. Take it. It's the C-40. The full twenty-two configurations." If I had passed my Ranger exam, I would've only gotten a C-10—like my sister's. Only advanced Rangers were cleared to access that many weaponry options. His cutlass could transform into basically any weapon I could imagine.

I accepted his cutlass, noticing how big it looked in my thirteen-year-old hands, how much heavier it felt than any of the others I had held. I locked eyes with my father, not ready to turn away. We both knew this might be the last time we ever saw each other. The knowledge made me wish even more that we hadn't spent so much of my childhood apart. But there was no point in thinking about that now. All I could do was complete my mission so we could both have a second chance.

"This is not training," Dad reminded me, as if I weren't completely aware. "The threats you will be facing are real. Every single decision you make will be life or death. This is a Class-One Quarantined planet. Everything on this planet has evolved to kill humans." I looked at him in surprise, and he asked, "Do you know where we are?"

"No, sir," I replied.

"This is Earth, Kitai."

But how could we have ended up back here, when humans hadn't been near Earth since we left it over one thousand years ago? Out of everywhere in the whole universe, why did we have to land on the one planet that had turned on us and nearly killed us all? It seemed like a cruel joke.

The worst part, though, was knowing that the Ursa was out there somewhere. I shivered at the thought of it waiting for me. It had my scent, after all. I was the human it would hunt to the death, if it had survived the crash, if it had escaped. "The Ursa?" I said, and my dad understood exactly how terrified I was.

Cool as ever, my dad replied, "There are three possibilities. The first and most likely is that it died in the crash." I nodded, comforted by his words. He continued, "The second and less likely is that it is injured very badly and still contained. And the third and least likely is that it is out." He spoke with a calm certainty that steadied me, but I knew better than to simply hope for the best. My dad gave voice to that thought too. "We will proceed, however, in anticipation of the worst-case scenario. Every movement will be under protocol: escape and evade. If it is out there, I will see it long before it gets anywhere near you. Don't get ahead of yourself. Do everything that I say and we will survive."

I rushed forward and wrapped my dad in a hug. His shoulders were so broad, I could barely get my arms around them, but it didn't matter. He hugged me back, for what seemed like forever. This was the hug I had hoped for back at our apartment. Too bad it took almost dying to bring us closer.

Finally he said, "Time's wasting. And we've got a lot to do." I forced myself to pull away, doing my best to stand up straight and strong as I snapped my cutlass onto my backpack. "I estimate H plus four days to reach the tail," he told me. "Use your naviband. Stay on the trajectory I've plotted. The temperatures on this planet fluctuate dramatically daily and most of the planet freezes over at night. There are hot spots, geo-thermal nodes between here and the tail, that will keep you warm during the freeze-over. You must reach one of these nodes each evening before nightfall."

I gave him one last look before I managed a weak military pivot and left the cockpit.

I reached the air lock, and the first set of giant doors hissed open. I saw the first glow of light pene-trating the darkness, beginning to melt the ice on the windows. That seemed like a good sign, but I still felt terrified as I faced the hostile planet alone.

My training gave me a way through the fear. The key was to break things down into manageable steps. At least, in theory. I activated my naviband and asked, "Can you hear me, Dad? Over."

"Copy." His voice was clear and strong over the communicator. I drew strength from the sound of it.

Staring into the shadows outside the shelter of the ship, I pulled out the cutlass. It was the best tool I had, and I figured I would need to keep it ready. I tapped a combination on the handle, and it slid into a curved blade that nearly sliced into my lifesuit. Not the right combination, obviously. I only knew the basic configurations that Cadets use in training exercises. I had tried picking up some of the others from watching the Rangers, but clearly I hadn't gotten it exactly right. After I retracted the blade, I tried another pattern, and it extended to its full two-meter length, with razor-sharp ends. At least this configuration I knew.

Stepping out, I heard the sound of small stones falling in the cavern beyond. I drew a deep breath as the ship's doors ground closed behind me, then leapt down. The sight of Rangers dangling from their harnesses at the torn edge of the ship made me jump back. I stumbled, feeling like I might hyperventilate again. For just a second, I'd thought I could actually do this. But not one step outside of the ship and I was already losing it. This was never going to work.

Dad must have seen the spike on my vitals monitor because he said, "Kitai, take a knee."

This again. When I was little, any time Senshi or I got upset, our dad always told us to take a knee. It was his go-to method for calming us down. My sister had seemed okay with it, but I always felt like it was a waste of time. But now, I felt so out of control that it was a relief to drop to my knee.

"I want you to take your time," he told me. "Acclimate yourself to the environment. Tell me any and everything. No matter how inconsequential it may seem. Everything you see, hear, smell, how you feel. Over."

Once again, hearing his voice made me feel better. Looking up, I saw a patch of daylight above me. "My body feels heavier," I said.

"Very good," Dad replied. "The gravitational pull on

this planet is slightly different than at home."

That was a relief. I was thinking there was something wrong with me, some injury we had missed on the ship. Or that now that I was faced with a real mission, I was freezing up, nowhere near as ready as I had assumed back home.

I reminded myself to stop freaking out and deal with the small steps that would eventually carry me to my goal. Looking up, I saw it was about sixty meters to the top of the ravine. Dad told me to get going. "Roger," I agreed. Enough messing around. I couldn't afford to give in to my fear, not this time. Not with both our lives on the line.

I began climbing the wall of the ravine, carefully searching out hand- and footholds. No problem—standard rock-climbing. I was good at this. Near the top, I glanced at my right hand to see a huge spider perched on it. I screamed, flinging it from my hand. Losing my balance, I slipped before catching myself with my left hand.

"Kitai! What happened?" my dad shouted. I heard the worry in his voice and felt ridiculous. I hated spiders, that was all. Maybe because with all those creepy-crawly legs, they reminded me of tiny Ursa.

Stabilizing myself, I asked, "You didn't see that? I thought—"

But he interrupted. "What's your situation report?

Your vitals spiked."

That was when it hit me that despite what he'd said, I really was alone out here. It wasn't like having him with me. He wasn't able to see more than I could, as he'd promised. This mission's failure or success was completely on my back.

So I snapped myself back into control. "No change," I replied. "I slipped. I'm good to go. There's condensation on the stones. I'm fine." I lied without hesitation, and he didn't call me on it. Proving once again that he wasn't the all-powerful Commander General I had always imagined.

I finished my climb to the top, pulling myself onto an elevated plateau. Despite the exhaustion that was already dragging me down, I was blown away by the view spread out below me. The sky was streaked with the purple, orange, and pink of sunrise. Eagles soared overhead, and hundreds of buffalo roamed below. The animals' calls rang through the air. We had some of these creatures on Nova Prime, but others hadn't survived there—those I only knew from history books, though they had clearly evolved since we'd been gone. I had always thought of Earth as a wasteland that we fled when it could no longer support life. Yet here it was, full of vibrant colors, scents, and sounds. I guess humans really were the problem. Without us, the planet appeared to have healed itself.

While I soaked up the view, my dad was planning my route. "There is an escarpment where two Earth continents collided. Looks like it could be a waterfall. It's at about forty-five kilometers. We'll call that our midway checkpoint. There's no way you can return after that. We'll assess rations and reevaluate when you get there. But let's break it into sections. First leg is twenty kilometers to the mouth of the north forest." Which reminded me that although I was technically out here alone, I was still lucky to have my dad there to oversee the mission. No way could I have come up with a plan like that. I memorized his instructions, since I knew my life would probably depend on them.

Glancing at my naviband, I saw that my holographic map also reflected what he had said. "Let's take it easy. Set chronometer for one hundred eighty minutes."

I didn't see the point to taking it *that* easy, though. And yeah, I wanted to show him what I could do. "One hundred eighty minutes? That's not right. I can do ten K in fifty minutes. You'll see." After checking my map, I started a light jog in the direction Dad had chosen. It felt so good to be running again that I added, "I might even do it in under forty minutes."

When he didn't answer, I slowed down, worried that something had gone wrong back at the ship. "Dad, do you copy?" More silence. I stopped, my concern growing. I knew how badly he was hurt. What if he had passed out, or worse? "Dad, do you read me? Over." Again, nothing. Now I was panicking. How was I supposed to do this without him? I couldn't. It was impossible. "Dad, do you copy? Are you there?" I was shouting now, desperate for some response. "Dad, I'm coming back," I called, already running back toward the ship.

"No need," my dad replied, his tone cool. "You just go ahead."

I slid to a stop, relieved but confused. "Huh?"

"Seems to me that you're in charge of this mission. And in my limited military experience, when two people are in command, everybody dies. So I will defer to your leadership, Cadet." He didn't sound mad, but I knew I was in trouble.

"Dad, I was just saying—" I protested, but he cut me off.

"What is my name?" he demanded. I stayed silent, unsure of what he wanted from me.

"What is my name?" he repeated, louder this time.

Shaken by his sudden fury, I replied, "General Cypher Raige."

"And who am I?" he asked.

"Commander General of the Rangers." My voice was barely above a whisper.

"That is correct!" he shouted. "And from this second forward, you will refer to me as 'Sir,' 'Commander,' or 'General'! You will follow my every command without question or hesitation. Am I crystal clear, Cadet?"

I had never heard my dad lose his cool before. I snapped to attention and barked, "Sir, yes sir!"

His voice even again, he responded, "Now at H plus one-eighty I need you at that forest. Set your chronometer."

"Sir, yes sir!" I set my chronometer and began to walk. Striding along a ridge, I looked over green fields that seemed to go on forever and a valley covered with wildflowers. Despite everything, it was pretty amazing to be here on this planet.

I would stay on his route now. I had wanted to go faster, to try to get him help sooner. But I really hadn't been trying to subvert his command. I didn't understand why he had reacted like that, except maybe that he wasn't used to anyone contradicting him ever. Or he just wanted to put me in my place, remind me that I'm just a kid. Or he was frustrated, trapped back there on that ship while I was out here, taking all the real risks. But I knew now that I'd better not step out of line again. Not for a while at least. And not with him.

Since I'm alone out here, I figure I might as well try to get some of this recorded. It is my first mission, after all. Hopefully the first of many. Or if everything goes sideways, maybe it will be a record someone

finds someday, to tell them what became of Earth—
and of me.

As I watch clouds sweeping over the mountains and
fields around me, my dad—I mean, *the Commander
General*—says, "Standard operating procedure till I give
you further instructions."

"Copy." It would've been nice to have a dad I could
actually talk to on the other end of the line, just to pass
the time if nothing else. Sure, I'm lucky to have access
to his military knowledge and experience. If anyone
can help me survive this, it's him—I know that. But why
couldn't he be awesome at his job *and* a decent father?
He was to Senshi. But he never has been to me.

So there's nothing to do but run to blot out the pain
of the distance from my father, and the feeling that he
doesn't even want to know me. I'm not going anywhere
near as fast as I could, since I know he doesn't want
me to, but the steady rhythm of my feet pounding the
ground calms me. Adjusting my stride to adapt to the
changing terrain, I chant to myself, "Who wasn't advanced to Ranger? Watch him go! Watch him go!"

My thoughts wander to my first memory, back
when I was only three. I was marching around our old
apartment in my pajamas and my dad's huge boots,
struggling to hold his cutlass. My sister must have
been off at Ranger training already.

"Those lines are tight, son," Dad told me, and I felt

pride and happiness like I have never felt since. My smile on the video my mom made is blinding. I ran over and hugged my dad, feeling incredibly safe and warm.

"And now it's time for one junior officer to head off to bed," he said.

"Noooo," I protested in my little-kid whine.

"That's a direct order from a superior officer, son." At that, I straightened up and gave him a salute. Dad leaned down, his face serious as he said, "We never disobey an order. Not at home, not when deployed."

"Yes, sir!" I agreed.

"And give your mother a kiss, tell her you love her." As I did, I heard him say to her, "One day, I'm just going to be known as 'Kitai's dad.'" He sounded so proud.

I've thought about that memory over and over again. It's the best proof I have that he used to believe in me, used to think that one day, I would be greater even than him. I remember being in that moment, feeling so grown-up carrying my dad's cutlass, yet so aware of what big boots I had to fill. And so confident that I could do it, one day.

But living in the past doesn't do any good. Maybe this shipwreck, horrible as it was, has finally given me another chance at a relationship with my dad. After a while I ask, "Hey, Dad, you there?" just to hear his voice again.

It takes him a moment to answer. I thought I'd

done something wrong again, but I guess he was just checking our plan. "Cadet, the Earth's rotational cycle is shorter than back home. You have six hours to reach the first geothermal site."

"Roger." Making my way along a jagged fissure in the ground, I see rocks jutting up toward me from the darkness below. It looks like a giant reached down and cracked the ground open like a giant egg.

"Let's stay in the shade as much as possible," my dad adds. "Direct sunlight is intensely carcinogenic. You must limit exposure." I'd thought the sun felt really intense, but with this info, I darted to a patch of shade.

"The rain used to be acidic, but it doesn't seem to be a problem now." That was a relief, at least. The sun could kill me, but the rain probably wouldn't.

Making good progress, I soon reach the edge of the forest. I see trees spilling over seemingly endless valleys. "Twenty kilometers, one hundred eighty-four minutes. Request breather, Da—I mean, sir."

I'm surprised when he replies, "Negative. You've got three hours to reach the hot spot. That's plenty of time. Hydrate now and keep moving." It's not like I need a break—I just wanted to check out the view for a little while longer, since I have plenty of time.

But he must have his reasons, and he made it clear it's not my place to question him. That doesn't mean I have to like it, but I swallow my annoyance and do as I

was told. I flip open a hydration tube and drink it down as I enter the forest.

The trees are insane. Ninety meters high, six meters in diameter—unbelievably big. I make my way carefully through the shadowy forest, peering into the foliage that surrounds me. But suddenly, I see that my lifesuit has turned jet black, its surface hardened and bumpy like armor.

I think it looks cool, but I figure it's not a good sign. I tell my dad, and he explains, "Your suit's made of smart fabric. It has motion sensors. I'm tracking a lifeform moving near you from the west."

Tensing, I whisper, "Ursa?"

"Negative. It's smaller. Bio-signs read only a meter and a half long." He says that like it's no big deal, but I freeze.

"*I'm* a meter and a half long!" If the smart fabric thinks this thing is a threat, who am I to disagree? I want to run, but my dad starts rattling off instructions.

"It's closing rapidly from the west. Do not move. Relax. Try to give me visual. Creatures on this planet have evolved from the ones we have on record because of radiation bursts. It's at fifty meters, forty, thirty . . ."

My breath comes ragged and fast. I better stop recording and get ready to fight. More later—I hope.

Well, I survived. Not without some damage. But we'll get to that.

My dad told me the thing was slowing down. "Twenty . . ." While he paused, I hoped that the thing had changed direction. But then he resumed counting. "Ten . . ."

I prepped myself as best I could, holding my cutlass out in front of me. But as I listened to plants snapping beneath the approaching creature's feet, it got harder and harder not to completely freak out.

"It's right there, Kitai," my dad said quietly.

"I don't see it! I don't see anything," I said in a panicked whisper.

"Relax, Cadet. Recognize your power." His words calmed me somehow, though I didn't really understand what he meant.

Slowly, an animal that reminded me of the baboons I'd seen in pictures appeared. Primates other than humans hadn't done well on Nova Prime, so I had never seen one up close before. Its face was strangely human, but it walked on four feet.

"It's fine, Kitai," my dad said, watching the primate on the video feed. "Be still. Let it pass. Do not startle it."

But I doubted he could see the way it was looking at me, the threat I saw in its eyes. I didn't think I could just wait for it to go away. It seemed like it was looking for a fight.

I picked up a nearby rock and brandished it at the baboon. Now I was razor-focused on the beast, blocking out all other sights and sounds.

"Back up!" I shouted. The creature screeched in response, but didn't move away. I waved the rock at it again, more threateningly this time.

"Don't do anything!" my dad ordered, but I didn't listen—couldn't listen. He wasn't out here—he didn't see how dangerous this beast was. "Kitai, no!"

"Get out of here!" I yelled as loud as I could, hoping to scare the thing away.

I heard my dad cry, "Kitai, stop!" but it was too late. I had already released the rock, which just barely hit the baboon. I wasn't trying to hurt it—I just wanted it to get away from me.

"You are creating this situation," Dad said. "Be still." I knew he could see my vitals skyrocketing, but I thought my way had worked.

Then a bunch of baboons burst out of the brush, their bloodcurdling war cries echoing through the forest. "Cadet, get control of yourself!" my dad shouted. "Listen to my instructions!"

With the creatures surrounding me, I tapped a pattern on the cutlass's handle. The fibers at its ends retracted into the handle and disappeared. I stared at it in shock. That wasn't at all what I had wanted. Looking up, I saw the baboons closing in. Panicked, I tapped out another pattern. The handle separated to form two batons. That would do. I swung them all around me to fend off the beasts. But they jumped out of range, then advanced again.

"To your rear, Cadet!" my dad shouted. "Out to your rear!"

Glancing behind me, I saw the opening my dad had seen and made a break for it. I attached the cutlass to my back and ran as fast as I could. The baboons chased me while I darted through the forest. Good thing I'm fast. I leapt from rock to rock and sprinted through the dense forest, outrunning them.

But then they swung into the trees and started gaining on me. That was one technique I couldn't match. They grabbed large pinecones from the trees and hurled them down at me. More of them were joining the chase every second. I counted ten, then twenty, then fifty of the creatures, all swinging and jumping through the trees, all throwing things at me. Somehow I managed to dodge everything they threw. Guess baboons don't have great aim. But eventually, one of them was bound to get in a lucky shot. A giant pinecone struck me square in the back, and I stumbled before turning the motion into a forward roll and springing back to my feet.

"Cross the river, Cadet!" my dad called over the noise of the chase. "I repeat, cross the river!"

I stopped short when I reached the bank of a raging river. The water was rougher than I had expected, but with the creatures screeching close behind me, I had no choice. I dove in.

From the shore, all fifty baboons continued throwing branches and pinecones after me, the water exploding around me with their projectiles. I was a strong swimmer, but bobbing in and out of the water to dodge their attacks was wearing me out fast. I gulped water, then burst back to the surface. I looked back, trying to see whether they were gaining on me, but there was water in my eyes and I couldn't get a clear view.

"Cadet, they are no longer in pursuit," my dad said.

Although I heard his words, they didn't sink in. Reaching the other side of the river, I scrambled out of the water and fled.

I noticed that my lifesuit had turned back to a rust color, but I wasn't convinced that everything was okay. "I say again, they are not following you," my dad repeated.

I didn't believe him. I ran as fast as I could, every noise in the trees driving me to go even faster and farther, certain that the beasts were closing in on me. "Cadet, you are not being followed!" he insisted. "Kitai, you are running from nothing!"

Reaching a clearing, I slowed to pull out the cutlass. I executed a 360-degree turn, bracing myself to fight off whatever came at me.

"Put my cutlass away," my dad ordered. "Take a knee, Cadet."

I finally obeyed, dropping to one knee, panting. My eyes were wide, darting frantically around the clearing; I was terrified that another attack was coming.

"If you want to die today, that's fine. But you are not going to kill me today. You are not out here by yourself. Everything you do affects me. I see right now that you do not have the intelligence to think for yourself, so I will be your brain. You *do not* think." I wanted to nod, but I felt foggy, frozen in place. He was right. I couldn't think. It would be a relief not to have to.

"Kitai, I need you to do a physical assessment," my dad said. I registered the concern in his voice and thought that was nice until he said, "I'm showing rapid blood contamination. Are you cut?"

I'd been fighting, running, swimming—but I hadn't been cut. I would've remembered that. Curled in on myself, I noticed that my lifesuit had turned white. I didn't know what white meant.

"Kitai, I need you to do a physical evaluation! Are you bleeding?" His stern voice broke through my shock.

Slowly I started doing an assessment, but when I tried to stand, I staggered, off balance.

"Kitai?" my dad asked, the concern there again.

"I'm dizzy," I said. The words didn't sound right to me. My lips felt swollen.

"Check yourself," he insisted. I looked down at my hands and saw a giant leech-like parasite attached to my left hand. I ripped it off, disgusted, and flung it away. But it tore my skin as I did, and a nasty rash bloomed where the thing had been.

"Open your med kit, Kitai." My dad's voice was ultra-calm.

I reached for my backpack, but I was so tired, and it was just out of reach. Gathering all my strength, I scooted forward and managed to loop my finger around it. "I can't stand up," I muttered. My fingers felt thick, and I fumbled with the med kit before finally managing to open it.

"You have to administer the antitoxin in sequence," my dad said, his tones smooth and comforting. "Inject yourself with the clear liquid first." I nodded, staring at the syringe, but couldn't remember how to use it. "Do it now!" he shouted when I paused too long, breaking his calm to get my attention.

It worked. I popped the protective cap off the first hypodermic needle. My hands shook, but that wasn't my biggest problem. "Dad," I said. "I can't see."

"The poison is affecting your nervous system," he explained. "Relax. Stay even."

I didn't see how relaxing would help when I was going blind. I fumbled with the needle, my eyes swelling shut. I knew I couldn't afford to panic, but I couldn't help it. "Dad, please come help me," I cried out like a little kid. I knew it was impossible, but it was also impossible for me to save myself. "I can't see! Please come help me!"

"Stay even!" he insisted. "Inject yourself directly into the heart with the first stage now!"

Taking a deep breath, I stabbed the needle into my chest and pressed the plunger down.

"Now the second stage," Dad said. "Hurry."

Fumbling blindly, I searched the med kit for the next needle.

"Your left, to your left!" Dad called. I was grateful that the video feed was still working.

After what felt like way too long, I found the second hypodermic. My eyes were completely swollen shut now, my hands shaking, but I managed to remove the needle's cap by feel. I stuck the needle in, but my thumb wouldn't move to press the plunger down. "I can't feel my hands! I can't . . ."

Darkness rolled over me in waves, but I fought to stay conscious. As I fell to my knees, I heard my dad say, "Press it into the ground! Kitai, roll over on it and press it into the ground!"

With the very last of my strength, I threw myself forward and felt the medicine burn into my chest as the plunger hit the ground. I slumped over and lay limp in the grass, barely conscious and unable to move.

"Great work, Cadet. Now you're going to have to lie there." That I could do. "The parasite that stung you has a paralyzing agent in its venom. You're just going to have to lie there for a little bit while the antitoxin does its job."

//////// ENTRY 9

I lay there forever. I felt like I was drifting but I also felt very, very heavy. It seemed like the world was getting darker and colder with each passing moment. I thought death might feel like that.

"Kitai." My dad's voice seemed to be coming from far away. Then I remembered, he *was* far away, alone on a ruined ship just like I was alone in this empty clearing. I thought about answering, but my lips wouldn't move. Or maybe I just drifted off again before I could try.

"Kitai, it's time to get up." I thought I heard some fear in his voice now, but that was impossible. The great Cypher Raige is one of only seven humans in history to be completely free of fear. Maybe I was dreaming. Maybe in the dream, my dad loved me so much that his worry for me was greater than his unbreakable, inhuman composure. Something howled around me—

maybe the wind, maybe a wolf. Nothing I could do, either way.

"Kitai, I want you to blink your eyes." I just wanted to sleep, but he wouldn't leave me alone. "Son, I need you to please blink your eyes."

That was strange. He hadn't called me "son" in years. I had to know if I had imagined it, so I fluttered my eyes open. "Hey, Dad," I said, my voice raspy and throat dry. "That sucked."

"That is correct." I wondered if I had just heard my dad attempt a joke. Not at all what I expected from him. But then he continued drily delivering the facts, and I figured things were back to normal. "The temperature is dropping five degrees every ten minutes," Dad told me. "You've got twelve kilometers to the hot spot." No time for a heartfelt reunion, then. Back to business.

Struggling to my feet, I began gathering up my gear. When I finally had everything, my dad said, "Let's see that ten kilometers in fifty minutes that you spoke about earlier, Cadet."

Of course, that was my speed when I was feeling good. Now I felt terrible, still recovering from the leech's poison, but I had no choice but to try. If I couldn't get to the hot spot in time, I would freeze—simple as that.

"Sir, yes sir," I said, my voice still weak and raspy. Setting my naviband, I followed its bearings to the north. I sprinted unevenly over the icy terrain. I saw animals scrambling underground to avoid the deep freeze. Then it started to snow, and I drew in a breath as the tiny ice crystals brushed my bare head and cheeks.

When my dad asked for an update, I told him, "Ten mikes out. Good. All good." I ran steadily, though it took everything I had to simply keep putting one foot in front of the other as the cold seeped into my body. "Five mikes out," I reported, feeling pretty proud of myself for shaking off the poisoning and running through the freezing air.

I arrived at an elevated volcanic area where steam rose from the ground. Lush trees lay tipped over with the weight of overripe fruit, the sickly sweet scent of rot filling the air.

"Hot Spot One arrival," I announced. "H plus forty-eight minutes!"

Outside the geothermal zone, I saw that the entire forest was covered in ice. Coughing, I said, "Sir. I made it. I'm here."

It took him longer to answer than I would've expected, and I wondered again if everything was okay back on the ship. But when he replied, he sounded as in control as ever. "Make sure you have everything. Take your next inhaler. Your oxygen extraction is bottoming."

I opened the med kit to do as he said, but what I saw was beyond belief. Terrifying. Life-threatening.

Two of the five remaining vials were broken. I didn't know if I had crushed them in my fight with the baboons, or maybe when I fell over after the leech poisoned me, but it didn't matter. All that mattered was that I didn't have enough breathing fluid left to complete my mission. Technically, that meant the mission should be over, right now. I hid the kit from my dad, not wanting him to know we were doomed. I would find some way to make it work—I had to. Both our lives depended on it.

"Use the next dose of breathing fluid," my dad insisted.

As another coughing fit threatened to overtake me, I realized that he was right—I was already struggling to breathe. But I wasn't going to let him see the trouble I was in, not if I could help it. "I'm good, Dad. I don't need it right now."

If I could hold out just a little bit longer with each vial, maybe I could stretch them out enough to make it to the ship's tail. There were probably med kits there, where I could get more breathing fluid for the trip back. I tried not to think about how much worse the crash had probably been for the tail section of the ship, how there might not be any usable med kits left.

I expected my dad to argue, but he just said, "Okay."

It felt like my chest was being crushed, and I kind

of wished he would yell at me to take the next vial until I had no other choice. Then it wouldn't be my fault if I ran out before completing my mission.

Except that it would be, of course, since I was the one who had somehow shattered the vials. And I would die just as surely if I ran out of oxygen a little farther down the road as I would if I did it right now. I struggled to draw in a breath, coughing and wheezing as I did. The coughs built, racking my whole body.

I understood why they said Earth could no longer support human life. We couldn't breathe here without supplementing the oxygen supply. All these plants and animals had somehow adapted, but it seemed like a fair bet that humans would have just died out when our air supply tanked before we ever had a chance to evolve. I had never thought about breathing before— who does, when we do it automatically, every moment of our lives? But now it was all I could think about, and despite my efforts to conceal my pain, I doubled over. I stared at the vials, knowing that I could end my suffering now, but the thought that these few extra moments might make a difference in whether or not I survived kept me from doing it.

Finally, I couldn't hold out any longer. I pulled out the second vial of breathing fluid and inhaled it. Soon my labored breathing eased enough for me to say, "Second dose of breathing fluid complete."

"Count off remaining so you can keep track." Maybe I imagined it, but I thought he sounded satisfied. As if he sat there, quiet, to teach me some kind of lesson. I couldn't tell him that I was low on breathing fluid. He would never let me keep going, and I knew I couldn't stop.

So I choked out a lie. "Four vials remain, sir." He didn't call me on it.

I ducked into the musty hollow of a rotting tree, wanting to hide from a cluster of strange creatures. It was a good thing too, because I'd only just taken cover when the sky burst open, pouring down the hardest rain I'd ever seen. The tree offered some shelter, but not enough to completely protect me from the rain's stray splashes and spatters.

Shivering and exhausted, I looked up at the giant leaves above me and saw a bee caught in a spider-web. It tried to escape, making the gossamer thread that held it tremble. A spider bigger than my fist rushed down the web and started further entangling its prey.

I wasn't scared of much, but I was scared of spiders, and I almost looked away right then. But the bee was still fighting, and I hoped it would win.

When the bee stopped struggling, the spider seemed unable to find it, blind as an Ursa without fear to guide it. I watched as the spider went in for the kill, its venomous fangs bared—but then the bee snapped to life once more, stinging the spider again and again. It was wild, and savage—and amazing. The spider made its sluggish way to the center of its web to die, while the bee, still tethered by the web, gave up trying to escape and died too. Maybe it was just because I was tired and lonely, but the whole thing struck me as such a tragic waste. Was that what we were doing as we battled the Ursa—killing them, maybe, but also destroying ourselves? It all seemed so pointless all of a sudden.

"Dad?" I called over my comm unit. "Dad?"

"I'm here." It sounded like I had woken him up, but he snapped quickly to attention.

I could tell he thought something was wrong, and I felt bad for worrying him just because I was miserable and bored. But since he was up now, I figured I might as well say what I had only now worked up the courage to ask. "How'd you do it? How'd you first ghost?"

I wanted to know so I could do it myself, of course. But I also thought that understanding this about him might give me a key to understanding *him*.

I expected him to tell me this was no time for stories, that I needed to focus on surviving and if I made it, maybe he would tell me. But he started talking right away, as if he'd been waiting for me to ask. It was probably pretty lonely back on the ship too. I hadn't thought of that before now—I'd been so focused on my own loneliness.

"I went out for a run. Alone. Something we're never supposed to do. Ursa de-camos right in front of me. I go for my cutlass. Ursa shoots its pincer right through my shoulder." The way he was talking, it seemed like he was still there, facing the Ursa. I wondered how often he relived that moment. Maybe constantly.

"Next thing I know, we're over the cliff. Falling thirty meters, straight down into the river. We settle on the bottom. It's on top of me, but it's not moving. And I realize, it's trying to drown me. I'm thinking I'm gonna die. *I'm gonna die.* I can't believe this is how I'm gonna die. I can see my blood bubbling up, mixing with the sunlight shining through the water, and I think, *wow, that's really pretty.* And everything slows down, and I think, *I wonder if an Ursa can hold its breath longer than a human?* I look around and I see its pincer through my shoulder and I decide I don't want that in there anymore. So I pull it out and it lets me go, and more than that, I can tell it can't find me. It doesn't even know where to look. And it dawned on me: fear is not real. The only place that fear can exist is in our thoughts of the future. It is a product of our imagination. Causing us to fear things that do not at present and may not ever exist. That is near insanity, Kitai. Now do not misunderstand me: danger is very real. But fear is a choice. We are all telling ourselves a story, and that day mine changed."

It was an amazing story, but at the same time, it sounded like something I might actually be able to do. I thought it was time to change my story too. Maybe, like the Primus would say, this whole crash had a reason. Maybe this is my time to step up and become a real Raige.

I couldn't fall asleep. I couldn't stop thinking about what he had said. I wondered why he'd never told me before.

I keep talking, though, quietly so as not to disturb my animal friends.

I haven't drawn much since I started Cadet training. But back when I was a kid, and especially right after Senshi died, I used to draw all the time. I was trying to re-create her on paper, because despite all the photos and videos we had of her, I felt like none of them really captured her, not the way I remembered her anyway. I thought if I could draw her, it would be like getting a little piece of her back. It never worked, though—there was always something missing in my drawings, just like in the photos. I hope someday I'll get it right. Maybe practice really does make perfect— in drawing, in Ranger classes, and in getting through to my dad.

As soon as the sun was up, so was I. I was gathering my gear when I heard from my dad again. "Fourteen kilometers from the falls. That's our halfway checkpoint."

"Reading you," I replied before beginning my trek, slow and steady, feeling the weight of sleep deprivation pushing down on me with so far still to go. I hacked my way through the forest with the cutlass, but it felt so heavy. I stopped for some water and ate a nutrition bar from my pack. I should have slept more last night. I could barely think, much less move, I was so tired. But I had to do both anyway.

"Seven kilometers from the falls." *Thanks for the update, Dad,* I thought but didn't say. Every kilometer I completed felt like a small victory, given what I'd been through already and what I had left to do. So of course

I was keeping track of every single one myself.

Annoyed, I wadded up the bar's wrapper and tossed it on the ground. Then I felt like a jerk. Earth turned against us because we treated it so badly, and here I was, on-planet for a day and already making a mess again. I grabbed for the paper, but it blew away on a gust of wind. I'd almost reached it when another gust floated it into a thick patch of vegetation. I plunged in after it, finally retrieving it. But then I looked up to see that the forest had been trampled, trees ripped down. Dozens of baboons lay butchered on the ground.

"What could do this?" I asked my dad. I didn't want to say what I suspected.

"Double-time it," my dad replied. "We need to make it to the falls. Hurry!" No argument there. I walked quickly beneath the forest's canopy, looking around in hopes of spotting the attacker before it was on top of me.

An enormous *boom!* rang out, and I ducked, drawing my cutlass. "Volcanic eruption," Dad explained. "Twenty kilometers east. You're fine. Keep moving."

A volcano sounded a heck of a lot better than an Ursa. I guess the increased volcanic activity is courtesy of the global warming we humans inflicted on the planet. I reached a steep hill and carefully tapped a combination into the cutlass. This time, the pattern did what

I wanted, forming two picks that I could use to climb the hill.

I asked if there was anything behind me, and Dad said there wasn't. But I heard something and froze, listening. It sounded like static in the distance, and I thought it might be the waterfall. That would be a very good thing.

"You're close," my dad confirmed. "Keep hustling."

I climbed faster, digging deep, but the lack of sleep was catching up with me. Then I stepped out of the forest, pushing giant leaves aside, and found myself on a rocky ledge. I connected the cutlass back into one piece and snapped it onto my back. The sound of the waterfall was deafening. More birds than I'd ever seen before swooped and circled through the mist in giant flocks. We hardly have any birds on Nova Prime, and I'm fascinated by these graceful flying creatures.

"Inventory up," my dad ordered, and I slowly unloaded my gear.

"Roger. Food rations: half available. Flares: full. Med kit: half available." Everything looked good—except for the one thing I couldn't survive without. "Breathing fluid . . ." I considered telling the truth this time. Maybe he could help me find a solution.

But I knew if I told him, he would order me back to

the ship. I wouldn't be able to disobey. And then we'd have no chance of survival. So I said, "Breathing fluid: four vials available."

"Why are you not showing me the case?" my dad asked.

"What?" I asked, like I didn't know.

But this time, he wasn't giving up. "Show it to me now."

I had no choice.

I held it up, revealing the two remaining vials.

I expected yelling, but all I got was silence. After a long moment, I couldn't take it anymore. "I thought I could make it, sir."

"Abort mission, return to the ship. That is an order." At his words, I flashed on Senshi telling me almost exactly the same thing, right before she died. *"Don't come out, no matter what. That's an order."* With the same order, my dad was forcing me to stand by and watch his death too. If I didn't complete the mission, I didn't see how either of us would survive.

"No, Dad, we—I—can do it. I can, I don't need many. I can get across with just two." I'd been through too much, come too far, to give up now. And I'd rather die trying than die giving up. At least if I was still out here, maybe I could make it to the ship's tail somehow.

"You need a minimum of three inhalers to make it

to the tail. You've exhausted your resources." There it was again, that utter calm, even though he was basically sentencing us both to die.

"I can get across," I insisted. "I can do it with just two, Dad." Just this once, I needed him to believe me—to believe *in* me.

"The mission has reached abort criteria. I take full responsibility. You did your best—you have nothing more to prove. Now return to the ship."

I started pacing, struggling and failing to keep my emotions in check. "What was your mistake? Trusting me? Depending on me? Thinking I could do this?"

As if I hadn't spoken, he replied, "Now I'm giving you an order, to turn around and return to this ship." There it was, what I'd been trying to avoid: a direct order from my commanding officer. An order that I would not, *could not* obey.

"You wouldn't give any other Ranger that order," I said, pacing closer and closer to the edge of the waterfall.

"You are not a Ranger, and I am giving *you* that order." I didn't know if he was saying that because I was his only living child and he wanted to protect me, or because I was the one who had let his favorite child die.

Suddenly, I had to know, the one thing I had always wondered, every day since *that* day. "What was I supposed to do?" I was yelling and crying and I didn't even care how far out of control I'd spun. "What did you want me to do? She gave me an order! She said no matter what, don't come out of that box!" Catching my breath, I repeated, "What was I supposed to do? Just come out and die?" The water roared in my ears as I waited for the answer I hoped for, or the one I dreaded.

He gave me neither. "What do you think, Cadet? What do you think you should have done?" Again with that incessant, uncrackable calm. "Because really that's all that matters."

But that wasn't true, not for me. His opinion was all that mattered, all that had mattered since the day my sister died. I had wanted him to tell me it wasn't my fault, that I had made the right choice, that he was glad that I had survived. Furious at his refusal to give me that, even now, I shouted, "And where were you? She called out for you, she called your name! And you weren't there, 'cause you're never there!"

I stood at the very edge of the falls, staring down at the birds swooping through the mist. The water roared in my ears. "And you think I'm a coward?" I was sure that's what he thought of me, even if he wouldn't say it. "You're wrong! I'm not a coward! You're the coward! I'm *not a coward*!"

I took two quick steps and dove off the cliff, toward the water below. The ground disappeared behind me and I was in free fall. Arms outstretched, body floating downward—for one perfect moment, I was at peace. My lifesuit released fabric that stretched from my legs up to my arms, creating wings that let me soar on the winds. I had a moment to think that this might have been an amazing idea, instead of a terrible one.

But then my lifesuit turned black, just as I heard my dad shout, "Kitai, you've got incoming!"

Something struck me midair—a massive predatory bird that immediately circled around for another attack. "Kitai, dive! Dive!" I pulled my arms to my sides, legs straight as arrows, turning myself into a torpedo to slice more quickly through the air. Not fast enough, though. The creature's razor-sharp talons flashed past my cheek as it slammed into me again and I heard my dad, one last time, scream, *"Kitai!"* This time, the force must've knocked me out. Because everything went black for a while, though I'm sure I kept on falling.

I woke to the feeling of something pecking at my face. I brushed it away, opening my eyes to find a newborn baby bird, just under half a meter tall, nuzzling my face. Definitely the weirdest thing I've ever woken up to. I took in the crosshatch pattern of light through the tree branches that made up the giant nest where I sat. Yeah, I was actually *in* a giant nest, and more than a little freaked out.

The baby bird bleated at me, opening and closing its beak. I got the uncomfortable feeling that it was hungry, and that I had been brought back here to feed it.

Turning, I saw several eggs around me, all starting to crack open. More baby birds pecked their way out and unfurled their slicked-back wings.

As I backed away, I saw the massive mama con-

dor that had knocked me out of the sky. The longer I looked at her, the more terrifying she got. She stood two meters tall, her beak razor-sharp, her wings when she opened them spanning over four meters.

Scanning the nest, I saw my torn backpack lying in the corner, my cutlass still attached. I snuck toward it as the other newborn creatures began climbing out of their eggs. Just as I reached my gear, I looked down and noticed a dark shape creeping up the tree trunk. I couldn't tell what it was.

One of the baby birds toddled toward me, and I nudged it aside with my foot, focused on the approaching dark form. Another dark creature dropped from above, landing on the huge branch that supported the nest. My hands shook as I grabbed my cutlass and tapped in a pattern. It extended to its full two meters in length, a sharp spear point at one end, a flat blade at the other.

I raised my cutlass just as the branch began to shake. I saw the condor fighting a lion-like beast, which left me clear to escape. But then I saw more lions scaling the nest, and glanced back to the squawking newborns in the corner. I realized that I couldn't stand to leave them, not so soon after watching them be born, not while they were under attack by a swarm of beasts. So I stood in front of them, cutlass at the ready. A lion reached its huge foreleg through the branches, its claws just missing me, but slicing through my naviband. Suddenly, paws were breaking through all over the nest. I saw claws connect with a baby bird. Under the force of the attack, the nest began to tear apart. I stabbed through the branches at a lion and the point of my spear pierced its fur.

Suddenly a large piece of the nest broke off, taking a howling lion with it. Other pieces fell too, leaving the interior of the nest open to the invaders. A lion crawled in and sank its claws into a newborn condor. I stabbed the creature's arm and it recoiled, climbing back down. As more lions tried to crawl in, I spun my cutlass, slicing one's paw and scaring off others. "Leave them alone!" I shouted.

The mama condor clutched a lion by its hind leg, flapping her broad wings as she dragged the squirming beast off the branch and into the air. Then she dropped it, and I watched as the lion plummeted to the earth far below. She did the same with another, but there were so many of them. One grabbed another newborn in its claws, and I rushed forward to stab the beast. It fell back over the edge, but it took the baby bird crashing down with it.

Now the condor and I were fighting off the last of the creeping lions. When the final one fell, I whirled, triumphant—and saw that not one baby bird remained. Only their shattered shells were left behind. The mama condor dove off the empty nest, and I thought she must want to escape the scene of the massacre. I couldn't unclench my hands from the cutlass, still scanning the nest, searching for another attacker, hoping for some sign of life in the ruins. But there was nothing.

Finally, I shouldered my gear and climbed down the massive tree trunk. When I reached the ground, I saw the mama condor hovering over a few of the lifeless chicks. She raised her head and shrieked up to the sky, the sound ripping through the forest. I knew she was just an animal, but I heard the grief in her scream— it was the sound I would have made, if I could have, when I watched Senshi die. Before I slipped into the jungle, I watched the condor touch her head to her chicks, then lift her head and scream again.

I'd felt her pain. As I made my way along the dense

jungle floor, I thought about the hatchlings that neither of us was able to save. I knew they were just birds, and I knew their mom tried to kill me first, and I knew it was the circle of life. But it wasn't really about the condors. It was about creatures with big claws and deadly intent creeping into your home and killing those who are too small and weak to fight back. How could I help reacting to the predators as though they were Ursa, and to the birds as though they were tiny and terrified eight-year-old me? So I had stayed, and I had fought, and still, I couldn't save them. The attackers were still too powerful, and I was still too small. Sure, this time I had helped beat back the attackers—but it still wasn't enough.

With my naviband damaged in the attack, I had even more reason to book it to the ship. It was my only chance of communicating with my dad, or anyone, again. Right then, I was more alone than ever. I ran through the jungle, hacking plants aside with my cutlass. All I could do was keep moving forward, and hope I was going in the right direction. I was sure I didn't have much time left. I had no idea how long I'd been knocked out in that nest. And fighting hadn't exactly been the best way to conserve my oxygen supply. I scrambled over rocks and fallen branches, crashed through underbrush, watched the sun dip dangerously low in the sky. I had to find a hot spot before I lost the light, or I'd freeze and no one would ever find me.

When I reached a plateau, I skidded to a stop and took in the ruins of what was maybe once a dam across a river.

A shadow passed over me and I looked up to see the mama condor flying recklessly, clipping treetops, dipping and weaving. As I watched, she rocketed straight up toward the sun. I watched her, and recognized grief that matched my own, and saw how pointless my behavior had been for so long. It finally struck me that the best way to honor my sister was to live as best I could—not to constantly risk my life just to prove I can. I saw the bird's suffering, how isolated she was by her grief, and it hit me how much harder it is to hurt alone. I had built up walls around myself to keep from ever again hurting as badly as I did when Senshi died. But it hadn't helped. I wanted to try a different path now. *I wanted to change my story.* I just hoped it wasn't too late.

I could see my breath, and I shivered as the temperature plummeted. Tired and lost, all I could do was run after the grief-stricken giant bird. Maybe she would lead me to a hot spot. But I didn't know how much longer I could keep going. I scanned the horizon for shelter, but saw none. The sun was dipping out of sight. I could see the plants curling in on themselves to protect against the night frost. Desperate, I turned left, then right, but there was nothing. So that was it,

then. Not how I expected things to go.

But then I saw a small hoglike creature running along, with three smaller hogs following it. It seemed to know exactly where it was going, so I followed it. The hog moved surprisingly fast, and it took all my agility to dodge under bushes, over rocks, and around tree trunks while keeping the small creature in sight. Finally I saw it burrow into a hole in the ground, and its babies scurried after it.

Without hesitation, I followed them. Except I didn't fit through the same small space. I found a flat stone and frantically dug at the hole until it was big enough for me to slide inside. I kept right on sliding, nine meters down till I had landed on a soft, grassy surface. It was pitch black, so I pressed my left shoulder to activate my lifesuit's light.

Looking around, I realized that the hog hole was actually a cave, its walls smooth stone. I crept between the narrow walls. I heard something slithering and watched a snake emerge from a seam in the wall. It spread its skin on either side of its body to form wings. As it floated through the cavern, I backed up against the wall, hoping it wouldn't notice me. I wasn't usually scared of snakes, but a flying one? That, I couldn't handle. I saw it swoop down on a rodent that was scurrying through the darkness and then lift its prey into the air.

My lifesuit's light revealed beautiful, multicolored cave paintings. I saw herds of bison on one wall, flocks of birds on another, a figure of a man sleeping, surrounded by a variety of animals. The paintings were crude, but majestic too. I knew they must be prehistoric, and wondered how long it had been since the last human saw them. They reminded me of the things I'd seen since I landed on Earth. They made me want to create a record like that of my own. Maybe that's what this recording is—and these sketches. Someday, someone might hear my words and see what I drew. Someday, someone might wonder who I am and how I survived.

At the bottom of the cave, I saw a tiny rivulet of lava winding through the darkness. I tried to quiet my mind, but it was racing. I settled in near the rivulet of lava to warm myself. But gradually, I began to feel confident that nothing was coming for me. I thought about the flying snake and the rodent—the circle of life, predator and prey.

But that's not the relationship between the Ursa and us. They were bioengineered specifically to hunt and kill us, by aliens we've never even seen. They are not our natural predators—they are killing machines designed to exploit our greatest weakness. It just seems so unfair—and yes, I know life isn't fair, but nature, in a way, is. Or should be anyway. Nature doesn't give the snake an unbeatable advantage over the rodent—it's just that that particular rodent didn't scurry quite fast enough.

But the Ursa were created for the sole purpose of eliminating humans, and when they weren't quite good enough at it, the Skrel redesigned them. I think we're on version six now, and they've got it pretty much right this time. Except that they never counted on my dad in all of their plans. He really is an anomaly.

Okay, he didn't save Senshi, he wasn't around much for me—but he did, in a very real way, save *humanity*. He singlehandedly canceled out a major chunk of that unfair advantage the Skrel gave themselves, yanking our battles with the Ursa back toward the natural order of things. Not all the way, not yet, but at least we have a fighting chance again. Maybe ghosting is how humans are evolving to combat the Ursa. Which makes me hope even harder that his skills have been passed on to me.

I found a piece of rock to make marks on the wall. Hearing my dad's voice in my head, I began trying to re-create the map he had showed me. I started with the ship, which I simply labeled *Dad*. Next, the forest where I battled the baboons. I remembered Dad's advice there, and how I didn't follow it. How I wish I had. Then the river that I crossed, the waterfall I leapt off of, the condor's nest. Of course that last leg was guesswork since I was unconscious for the flight from the waterfall to the nest, but I doubted the mama condor carried me very far. From there, I thought I knew the route I took through the jungle, though I may have been remembering it wrong. I drew the cave and marked it *I am here, I think.* Finally, I marked a large area on the left side of the map *Tail somewhere here.* I remembered how my dad entrusted me with this

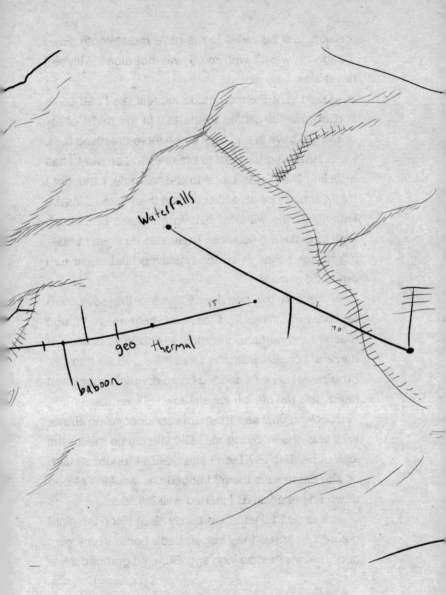

Waterfalls

15

geo thermal

baboon

40

mission, and his belief in me gave me strength. Even though he wasn't with me, I was not alone. Maybe I never was.

Looking at the map made me feel like I had some sort of plan for getting to the tail. In the midst of my drawing, I gave in and took some more breathing fluid. I was struggling too hard to breathe, and anyway, I had a feeling that I was close to the tail now. I thought I might actually be able to complete this mission. Maybe leaping off the waterfall helped me make up enough time to make a difference. There was no point in making myself suffer when the breathing fluid might turn out to be enough.

I noticed the hog family leaving the cave, so I gathered my things and followed them again. When I reached the surface, the mother hog looked back at me, and I could swear she gave me a nod, as if to say, "You're welcome." I nodded back, grateful. As she and her piglets ran off, a huge shadow fell over me.

Looking up, I saw the mama condor circling above. Why was she following me? Did she blame me for the loss of her babies? Didn't she realize I fought as hard as she did to save them? I hoped she wouldn't swoop down on me again as I started walking south.

I was dead tired. I had barely slept since the night before I boarded the Hesper, back home in my own bed. That seemed so long ago. Sure, I'd grabbed a few minutes of sleep here and there, and I'd blacked out a few times, but none of that had been exactly restful. Maybe I should have tried to get a full night of sleep in the cave, but mapping out my path seemed more important, especially since I was out of breathing fluid.

As I hurried through the jungle, I kept catching the condor swooping in and out of the treetops. I tried to stay hidden in the clusters of trees, but she seemed to have no trouble tracking me. "Leave me alone!" I finally shouted. But maybe she didn't hear me, or maybe she didn't care.

//////// ENTRY 12

I made pretty good time earlier, but I was still basically just dragging myself along. I almost got trampled by a bunch of animals that looked like horses or gazelles or something, until the mama condor grabbed my back with her talons and pulled me out just in time. I figure that's when I lost my cutlass. That condor was perched in the trees above me now, staring at me. She looked depressed, hanging her head, her wings drooping. I tried to keep my cool as I walked by, but I felt her watching me. And so I started to run, but pretty quickly ran out of juice. Really, I could barely walk. I was so tired. I didn't know how much longer I could go on. I mean, I wouldn't stop, not till I reached the tail or ran out of air. But I had almost nothing left.

Coming to a stop between two colossal trees, I

registered movement in their branches. There she was again. Still watching.

Eventually, I reached the bank of a river. I dropped my gear in exhaustion.

I sat for just a minute, battling the exhaustion that urged me to give up. It would have been so easy to just lie down there and go to sleep.

Noticing a log floating by in the river, I struggled to my feet and started cutting vines from the nearest trees, then gathered pieces of some fallen trees at the river's edge. Although my dad's cutlass was gone, I still had a knife stashed in my backpack, which worked for lashing together a basic raft. When it was finished, I pushed the raft into the river and jumped on board. The river was full of life, and I held my breath as a twelve-meter-long anaconda swam alongside me. But it passed quietly, and I relaxed. The current was strong enough that I didn't need to row, so I decided to lie down for a little while. The motion of the river soothed me and I closed my eyes, unable to fight the fatigue any longer. The chirping of birds and splashing of fish all around me was like a lullaby, urging me to sleep.

As soon as I fell asleep, I dreamed of Senshi. It felt so real that I wondered if I was actually dreaming, or if she really was—somehow—there. "Wake up," she said, touching my arm. I opened my eyes to see Senshi sitting beside me on the raft, her long hair hanging over her shoulder. She reached out to stroke my face, like she used to when I was little. I smiled up at my big sister, so happy to see her again.

"It's time for you to wake up," she insisted, but I shook my head. I was so tired and besides, I needed to talk to her. I couldn't go yet.

My throat felt dry, but I had to get the words out. "I was just about to come out that day."

She smiled. "No, you weren't. But you did the right thing."

I was glad to hear her say that, but still wasn't convinced.

"Why couldn't you ghost?" I asked her. I had always wondered that.

She just stared at me, then gently touched my face again. "You're close right now."

"I am?" That seemed impossible. Ghosting was hard, and I was too drained to do anything hard anymore.

"Are you scared?" Her voice was just as soothing and musical as I had remembered it.

"No. I'm tired." It was good to talk to her, but I wished she hadn't woken me up so soon.

"That's good. You filled your heart with something else. Now you've got to get up."

I looked up at her and said, "I memorized some of *Moby Dick*."

"Kitai, get up," she insisted.

I quoted some of the lines she had underlined, trying to keep her there with me, not ready to let her go.

But she kept interrupting, repeating, "Kitai, wake up." I wished she would stop pushing me. I just needed a little more time. "It's time for you to wake up."

I covered my ears and continued quoting the book that she and my dad had loved.

"Kitai, wake up!"

Senshi looked down, resigned, her hair covering her face. When she looked up again, her face was bleeding, just like it had that day. *"Wake up!"* she shouted, and this time, I did.

The river was already half-frozen. Senshi had been right—I had slept too long. My raft was docked against a riverbank. I sprinted madly for the jungle, with no idea where I might find shelter. As I watched the ice creep across the trees, I felt frost forming on my upper lip and the top of my head. My lifesuit turned white and iced over, but I kept moving. Shivering violently, I wrapped my arms around myself, hoping to preserve whatever warmth my body had left.

Hearing branches snap and crash to the ground, I looked up to see the condor above me, tossing the branches down. The jungle floor began to freeze and I collapsed to my knees. My face hit the cold, hard ground. I saw that my skin was turning blue. If only I'd listened to Senshi—who had tried to help me once more in my dream—I wouldn't be trapped there now. Maybe my dad and Velan were right—I didn't listen to anyone. I always thought I knew better. And once again, I'd been wrong. I felt ice forming on my eyelids and could barely see. Then the condor swooped down on me again, and everything went black.

I woke up buried under leaves and feathers. Sunlight flashed across my face but it was too bright, blinding. Shielding my eyes, I struggled to free myself from the ditch, crawling toward the light. Collapsing on the ground, I saw the ice beginning to melt, though it was still very cold. Somehow, I had survived till morning.

I turned to see the condor lying over the ditch where I woke. I saw that she had made a little nest for me, and kept me warm in it through the night.

"Hey," I said, tapping her, "thanks." But she didn't move. That's when I realized that she had sacrificed herself for me, allowing herself to freeze so she could keep me warm. I stood staring at the condor for a long moment, overwhelmed. She had given her life for me. Just like Senshi. How many others had tried to help me and I hadn't seen it? Emotions raced through me—guilt, sadness, but most of all, gratitude. Finally, I understood that no matter how isolated I might feel, I had truly never been alone. I turned and walked back into the jungle.

I followed a faint trail and found my way to a watering hole. I caught a glimpse of myself in the still, clear water, and was surprised by how much older I looked. Not just because of the stress I'd endured, but because of the knowledge and acceptance in my eyes. Finally, after the five years of struggle since my sister's death, I was at peace with myself. I felt at peace with this strange new world around me too.

As I scanned the jungle for any sign of where the tail had crashed, my breathing started to grow ragged. When I exited the jungle for a stretch of grassland, I began to cough. My throat felt raw as the coughs racked my body. The breathing fluid was almost completely out of my system. I dropped to my knees and caught a glimpse of something shiny in the tall grasses. I crawled toward it and saw a jagged piece of metal with the word *Hesper* stenciled on it. I ran forward, powered by my excitement, though each movement was a battle as my air ran out.

Spotting a small, spindly tree, I scrambled up to get a better view. I saw the enormous tail of the cargo ship, just up the hill, its reflective surface shimmering

in the sun. The tail section's crash had scorched a flat path through the terrain. I leapt out of the tree and struggled up the hill. Wheezing uncontrollably, I fought for every step. Ninety meters from the tail, I stumbled and fell. I clutched my chest, choking on the planet's air. Using my sleeve to cover my mouth, I staggered to my feet and kept moving.

I dragged myself into the wreckage and rummaged through debris in a desperate search for more breathing fluid. I fought back dizziness, my chest heaving, each breath ripping through my lungs. Light and dark whirled together as my vision began to fade and unconsciousness threatened to overtake me for the last time. But somehow, amid all the chaos, I found a container of breathing fluid still attached to a section of the wall. I fell to my knees beside it, tearing it open. I had never seen anything so beautiful. I managed to open a vial and inhaled the breathing fluid, feeling the oxygen fill my lungs once more. After pausing to catch my breath, I took another vial. I needed it. I fell on my back, gulping the precious oxygen.

Once my breathing steadied, I crawled to the cutlass rack and grabbed one. It felt good to be armed again. Now that I could breathe, I wanted to find out what had happened to the Ursa. As I ran through the cutlass's configurations, I scanned the area, trying to figure out what could have happened. From the damage to the surrounding trees and ground, I could see the path the ship's tail had taken when it crashed. Tracking the debris path, I headed down the slope, figuring that if the Ursa had been flung from the storage hold, the momentum would have carried it this way. My dad had said the Ursa was probably either dead or contained, and I could only hope he was right. I approached the Ursa's pod, my cutlass extended in front of me. As I circled around, I saw that the pod had been shattered.

Binding straps lay broken on the ground. I checked the area—no dead Ursa around. It had definitely escaped. Worst-case scenario.

But I had to focus on finding the beacon before I worried about the Ursa. As I searched the wreckage, I found a working naviband and snapped it on. Immediately, it began reading my vitals, and I tried to reach my dad. I'd been so busy trying to survive that I hadn't had much time to worry about him. But now, I could only hope I wasn't too late to save him. "Dad, are you there?"

All I heard was a lot of static. "Dad, I made it to the tail," I said, hoping he could hear me. I heard little bursts that I wanted to think were his voice, but nothing clear enough to be sure. Still searching the debris, I spotted the beacon and pulled it free. When I turned it on, I held my breath, hoping with everything in me that this one would actually work. It whirred to life, and relief washed over me. Except when I fired it, nothing happened. Fighting to stay calm, I stared at the beacon's screen. *Electrical interference*, it said.

I repeated my message, but still, no answer. Now the worry surged. I knew he was hurt bad. I knew I took longer than I should have to get to the tail. If only I had listened to him from the beginning. I could have followed his plan and gotten here sooner and we would both be safe aboard a rescue ship by now.

Repositioning the beacon, I tried again to fire it. And again, it *failed*. This stupid hunk of metal *failed*. "Dad, please copy," I said, my voice breaking. "Dad, you're still there, right? Can you hear me?" After everything I'd been through, I couldn't lose him too. Not now. "Dad, please—the Ursa is not contained!"

The rage and frustration welled up, uncontrollable—I'd fought so hard to reach the one thing that could save us, and now it wouldn't work. I gave in to my anger, throwing my backpack, screaming as I sliced into the ship with the cutlass. Whirling, shouting my fury to the sky, I threw the beacon to the ground, cutlass raised above it. But I stopped myself. Maybe there was still some way to make the beacon work. I couldn't give up, not after everything I'd been through. And although I couldn't hear my dad, I knew what he would say: "Take a knee." I could almost hear his voice as I dropped to one knee. For the first time, I wasn't doing it because he ordered me to. I was doing it because I knew it would help. I tried to think, wiping away tears, slowly pulling myself back together.

Looking up, I noticed the heavy cloud layer over me. It occurred to me that that could be the cause of the interference. If I could get above it, the beacon might be able to transmit. Scanning the terrain for a way to get up that high, I saw a black mountain in the distance, its peak above the cloud layer. Grabbing the beacon, I sprinted toward the peak.

In a clearing, I saw dead hyenas dangling from the trees. I hesitated, but there was no choice but to keep going.

Only one thing I knew of would've killed like that: the Ursa. I kept running, but now I was glancing around nervously, wondering where the monster lurked. But I knew that was what it wanted. It was trying to scare me, to make me release more pheromones so I would be easier to track. I wouldn't let it. I am Kitai Raige, son of Cypher Raige, and I was going to save both our lives.

When I reached the base of the mountain, I saw hundreds of bright red lava rivers rushing down its dark slopes. It was an amazing sight, and I was struck again by what a beautiful planet we humans nearly destroyed. Bursting out of the jungle, I ran up the slope, navigating between the slender ribbons of lava. I thought I heard something in the jungle behind me, but I kept moving. Fast and fluid now, revitalized by the infusion of oxygen. Soon I was inside the cloud layer, surrounded by a dense white mist. That's when I noticed that my lifesuit had turned black. I heard the scuttling of something approaching and brandished my cutlass. I couldn't see, though, so it wasn't like I could aim. Backing up, I found myself at the entrance to a cave. "Dad?" I said, hoping he could hear me now that I was near the volcano's peak. But still I got no reply. I knew the thing was close, though. Better stay quiet.

I hurried into the cave and found a tunnel covered in sparkling stones. Stalactites and stalagmites filled it, glittering in the light from my lifesuit. I ran deeper into the cave, not knowing if the Ursa was in front of me or behind me. All that mattered was that I knew it was coming for me. I searched for a way out of the cave, and saw a shaft of light beaming down from the ceiling. Suddenly, the Ursa decamoflaged right in front of me, and then leapt out of sight.

But I had seen an Ursa up close before, so the sight didn't freeze me in my tracks. I moved deeper into the cave. I navigated carefully around the spear-like stalagmites as a scream echoed through the cave—another way for the Ursa to frighten me. Except I had heard an Ursa's scream before, so it didn't startle me now. I ran as fast as I could on the uneven terrain, my cutlass extended. Ducking behind a thick stalagmite, I watched the cave's entrance. But I kept a clear sense of exactly where that shaft of light shot down from the ceiling, because that might be my only way out.

Scrambling low between stalagmites, I noticed a large crystal that had fallen across two rocks, and crawled beneath it. Eyes darting around the cave, I noticed dust dropping from above and I knew that was where the Ursa was. Just in time.

The Ursa leapt onto me, crushing the crystal that sheltered me. I was trapped now, its claws slashing toward my face. But as it moved around the debris, I was able to squirm out from under the crystal. I leapt to my feet, retrieved my cutlass, and whipped it around. The Ursa smacked me away, launching me three meters into the air. I landed on an outcropping of rocks, dazed. As I got back to my feet, I saw the beast use its hooked claws to push itself up and off the stalagmites that skewered it. Grayish blood oozed from its two wounds, dripping onto the floor.

I dove through a crevice that was too small for the Ursa. It screeched in frustration but then crashed through the crystals. I launched myself over another fallen crystal, but the Ursa clipped my leg with its claws, sending me rolling before I regained my footing. I slipped into a crevice and watched the beast. It stood there for a moment, then seemed to determine that it couldn't reach me and backed away. It camouflaged itself again to match the crystals and the rock wall, so I couldn't see it. As I crawled farther back into the crevice, I took my eyes off the space where the Ursa was just for an instant. I felt my terror threatening to overtake me. I knew how dangerous that was, but I didn't know how to stop it.

Then I heard the *drip drip drip* of blood falling to the floor, seemingly out of thin air. I'd found the Ursa.

It revealed itself, hanging upside down at the mouth of the crevice. It reached in, but its claws missed me. I warded off its attacks with my cutlass as I shimmied deeper into the crevice. The beast spit black globules at me, and I moved to avoid them. It spit again, and a glob hit my shoulder. It seared through my suit and into my skin like acid. I screamed, stumbling backward from the force of the gunk's impact. I slipped down a slanted slope, but the Ursa stayed with me, forcing its way past the crystals with every movement, but another globule made contact and knocked me over. Suddenly I was falling straight down through a shaft in the cave. I smashed into a rock, rebounding and falling farther, finally splashing down in a pool of underground water.

Underwater, I could only see about a meter in front of me using my lifesuit's light. I saw another shaft of light arcing down through the water. That meant there was another way out. I swam toward it, glancing back between strokes but not seeing any sign of the Ursa. Suddenly I realized that I was surrounded by strange fish that snapped their sharp teeth at me. They started tearing at my lifesuit.

The sound of something large splashing through the water scattered the fish. Out of the darkness, the Ursa's long claws reached for me. I swam away as fast as I could. I felt myself running out of breath, and desperately paddled toward the shaft of light.

In my frenzy to escape, I realized I'd lost track of which way was up. Blowing out what might be my last breath, I saw that the bubbles were going downward. I had somehow ended up upside down. Righting myself, I swam for the light. I emerged into a vertical shaft in the rock, gulping in air. Bracing my feet on either side of the rock shaft, I started climbing up toward the sunlight twenty meters above.

The Ursa erupted from the water, its claws snagging my legs. It couldn't fit into the shaft, so it tried to pull me down. I screamed as its long claws dragged down my leg, but I kept going. I got high enough that the Ursa lost its grip on me, crashing back into the water below. I kept pulling myself up the shaft, screaming in anger, screaming in pain, screaming in fear. It took all my strength to reach the top, but my fury propelled me. My hands grasped the top edge of the passageway, and I pulled myself up onto the side of the volcano. The ionic cloud layer was dissipating up here, but gray ash fell everywhere from an eruption at the top. There was nowhere to go. Peering back down the shaft I had just climbed, I saw rocks collapsing and knew the Ursa was coming. I had no time left. I took out the beacon, activating it, ready to send the rescue signal.

But just then, one of the Ursa's arms reached out of the hole and grabbed me, pulling my legs out from under me and slamming me into the ground. The beacon flew one way, the cutlass the other. Before I could react, the Ursa smacked me into another rock. I lay on my back, limp. Everything felt broken. I felt my blood seeping into the ground. I heard the Ursa scrabbling frantically to free itself from the shaft so it could finish the kill.

I reached for the cutlass that should have been on my back, but came up empty. I let my arm fall, noticing the falling gray ash making swirling patterns as it stuck to my skin, still wet from the water below. Images flashed through my head—the baboon meeting my gaze, the hog seeming to nod at me outside its hole, my sister's loving eyes as she turned away to face the Ursa, the mama condor fighting to protect her babies, the Ursa leaping for me in the cave, the Ursa leaping at Senshi in our old apartment, the bee jousting with the spider, Senshi in my dream of her on the raft, me crawling out from under the body of the mama condor, the bee ceasing to struggle, then breaking its bonds, my dad's voice saying, "Fear is a choice."

And then it all clicked, and my eyes snapped open at the revelation. My breathing slowed, the fear gone as I was filled with the warmth of all I had seen and experienced. The things where no one won—my battle with the baboons, the spider and bee killing each other, the lions killing the condor chicks while the mama condor and I killed them, the Ursa blindly attacking—these came from places of anger and fear. The things that were good—my sister saving me, the mother hog helping me, the mama condor protecting me, my father's words guiding me—these were all reminders that I was never really alone. If I was willing to accept it, there was always someone there willing to help. I wasn't alone. I never had been. And my dad wasn't alone either, not really. Not while I was still out here, still trying to save him.

The gray ash covered me, turning me into a different version of myself. Everything seemed to slow down. I felt completely at peace, at one with the mountain and the world around me. I heard the Ursa crash through the surface, but I was not afraid. The ash covered the monster too, keeping it from going invisible. It moved forward, but then it paused, looking lost. It moved around, searching for me, but it could no longer see me. I calmly got back to my feet and walked right past the Ursa to pick up my cutlass, and the beast didn't react. I stood staring at the monster for a long moment. Then I tapped a combination on the cutlass, and it split into two blades. I held them on either side of myself and ran at the Ursa, so fast and smooth that I was almost floating over the black rocks. The thing heard me coming, but it was too late. I leapt onto the alien beast's back and sank my blades into its two open wounds. The monster shrieked, writhing violently, but I held on. I tapped in another pattern, and the creature screamed as the cutlass extended into a spear and then a sickle, slicing the beast from the inside out. The Ursa staggered toward the cliff face, trying to take me over the edge with it. But I held tight until the monster fell. Then I stood atop the beast, swords at the ready, daring it to move. It did not. Lowering my arms, I gazed at the fallen Ursa with calm eyes. Snapping the cutlass back together, I jumped off of the beast and retrieved my backpack for the trek to the volcano's peak.

At this altitude, the freeze was already in full force. I hardly noticed the cold anymore. I felt strong again, my strides rhythmic. When I reached the top of the mountain, I turned the beacon on, holding it up to the sky. A bright white beam sliced through the night sky, up into space and out in all directions. Mission accomplished.

The rescue ship came quickly. As the crew prepared for takeoff, I headed to the control room to check on my dad. He lay on a cot with two medics beside him, both of his legs in braces. "Stand me up," he said.

"General—" the head medic protested, but my dad insisted. And when the Commander General gives an order, it's best to follow it. The medics helped him up, and I winced at the sight of his bandaged feet touching the floor.

My dad straightened up and, looking into my eyes,

raised his hand in a salute. I saluted back, feeling the understanding and connection passing between us. I walked over and gently hugged him, whispering in his ear. "Dad . . ."

"Yes?" he whispered back.

Grinning, I said, "I wanna work with Mom."

He chuckled. I hadn't been sure he still knew how to laugh. I hadn't heard him do it in years. Neither of us wanted to let go, but the medics gently separated us to lower my dad back to his cot. He needed his rest, and time to heal.

Through the ship's window, I watch a heavy rain fall around us. The ship begins to rise, higher and higher into the air, across the sky, out of the rain clouds. As we fly over the ocean, I see the tail of a huge whale-like creature disappear into the water of the deep blue ocean. The whale reminds me of *Moby Dick*. I think I get it now, what that book was really about. Captain Ahab went nuts after the whale took his leg. Senshi was like that to me, a part of me, a part I couldn't or didn't want to live without. When I lost her, I obsessed over becoming a Ranger as if that could fix it. I wanted to kill Ursa because one killed my sister, just like Ahab wanted to kill the whale because it sank his ship. My single-minded focus kept me from listening to anyone—my mom, my dad, Bo, Velan. Obsession blinds you. You zero in on one thing and miss everything that really matters. Like a mother who loves you, friends who care about you, the memory of a sister who wanted you to live, not die. And a father you've always admired, but are just now, finally, getting to know.

Of course, that isn't what the book meant to Senshi when she and our dad read it together. I pored over the passages she'd marked, trying to figure out what it had meant to her, so I'd know what it was supposed to mean to me. I guess I thought there might be some message there that would give me a way back to my dad's heart. But in the end, I had to forge my own path. Senshi lives on in our memories—mine, my mom's and my dad's—not in the crinkly, browned pages of an old book. My dad and I had to find our way together in the real world, not by reading about something that never even happened. And yet, the book taught me more about myself than any of the training manuals I've memorized ever could. I can see why our ancestors saved *Moby Dick* and a few other Forever Books, making room for these relics on the crowded arks that let humanity escape from our dying home planet. And now that I've seen Earth, I can see that it's better off without us. The plants and animals there have thrived, despite all the damage we did. Now it's up to us to take care of our new home, Nova Prime, so we never have to flee again.

I'm ready to go home. I'm returning as a Ghost, the

youngest one ever, but that's not what matters to me anymore. What really matters is that, down there, my dad and I found our way back to each other. That's all I ever really wanted.

I press my hand to the glass to bid the whale and its planet good-bye before we're out in space, surrounded by the stars once more.